# Grave Survey

## *Doug Fletcher book 10*

## *Dean L. Hovey*

Print ISBNs
Amazon Print 978-0-2286-2018-1
LSI Print 978-0-2286-2019-8
B&N Print 978-0-2286-2020-4

*BWL Publishing Inc.*

*Books we love to write ...*
*Authors around the world.*

http://bwlpublishing.ca

Copyright 2022 by Dean Hovey
Cover art by Christine's Cover Creations

All rights reserved. Without limiting the rights under copyright reserved above, no part of this publication may be reproduced, stored in or introduced into a retrieval system, or transmitted, in any form, or by any means (electronic, mechanical, photocopying, recording, or otherwise) without the prior written permission of both the copyright owner and the publisher of this book.

I0591985

This book is a work of fiction, a product of the author's imagination. Any resemblance to actual events or people is coincidental and unintended. Some actual locations are used fictionally.

Thanks to my legion of subject matter experts, beta readers, proofreaders, editor, cover designer, and publisher who all collaborate with me to make these books a reality. Julie puts up with my hours on the computer and my distant stare as the characters reveal themselves and the plot to me. Deanna Wilson has evolved from my horse and cop consultant into the expanded role of early proofreader, commenting on the plot and characters, often a few out of context pages at a time. Fran Brozo, Mike Westfall, Clem MacIlravie, and Brian Johnson offer plot critique and are my muses when I've written myself into a corner. Anne Flagge and Natalie Lund proofread and correct my numerous typos and grammatical errors. Susan Davis provides invaluable editing and supportive commentary. Jude Pittman, of BWL Publishing, has been marvelously supportive in getting my books into the hands of my readers. Most of all, thanks to you, the readers who provide me with feedback, plot ideas, and the energy to write.

# *Dedication*

*To Karla and Randy Tschetter*

# Chapter 1

Mike Lawler and his partner, Terri Smith, were packing their surveying gear in the truck when they heard a vehicle. Terri turned in the direction of the engine noise, pulled back her dark hair, and redid her ponytail. Her dark skin glistened with sweat as she watched the rutted trail for the approaching vehicle.

Nodding toward the single-lane driveway, Mike said, "I'll bet you ten bucks it's one of the drilling foremen. He'll ask again when they can start working on this site."

Packing the laser transit in its padded aluminum case, Terri replied, "Nah, I think it's the oil company rep, some goofy protesters, or the park ranger. We talked to the foreman this morning."

Slowly coming into sight through the cypress trees, a pickup stopped in front of Terri. Backlit by the afternoon sun, a man got out of the pickup, casting a long shadow in the waning daylight. He spat a stream of tobacco juice into the swamp alongside the road.

"We got a problem, Lawler," the man drawled.

Mike drew a breath in frustration. "I told you, I only mark the boundaries. I'm not the one who defines the property lines."

The man stepped from behind the pickup door, a holster dangling ominously from his belt. "You should rethink that position." His hand rested on the butt of the pistol.

Mike raised his hands. "Take it easy. We can talk this out."

Terri panicked at the sight of the gun. She turned and scrambled for cover on the passenger's side of their pickup. There was a flash of silver before the deafening sound of the gunshot. Dozens of roosting birds burst from the canopy of trees, cawing their displeasure.

"What the hell?" Mike yelled as he rushed to Terri's aid. He fell to his knees next to her as she crawled ahead, leaving a trail of blood in the grass. When she collapsed, he rolled her over. Her desperate eyes searched his face for an answer about what had happened. Her lips moved, but no sound came out. A stream of blood pulsed from her chest, spreading crimson on her shirt. Mike fumbled with his phone. "I'm calling an ambulance!"

"There ain't no point. You'll both be dead before anyone answers."

A deafening shot preceded the searing pain in his back, Mike felt like someone had punched him hard enough to knock the wind out of him. He looked down at the blood flowing from a hole in his shirt and comprehended what had just happened. He knelt and hovered with a hand over the spurting blood and then tumbled forward. His vision went dark as life leaked from his body.

The shooter fired another shot then holstered his gun and turned to his partner. "Don't just stand there. Let's load them into the back of their truck. You drive it out of here."

# Chapter 2

After completing our Everglades National Park investigation, Jill rebooked our return flights to Texas. We found a beach hotel overlooking the Gulf of Mexico, bought beachwear, and became tourists. Jill had gotten emotionally keyed up after the arrest in Belize. It had taken three sleepless nights spent pacing the floor and pulling up internet stories on her cell phone before she'd been able to sleep for even a few hours without waking to a nightmare.

Jill decided to skip her bedtime wine after viewing our fourth incredible sunset from our balcony at the Sanibel Island hotel. We slipped into bed, and she snuggled into my shoulder, sleeping through the night, although I figured the nightmares were still there because she twitched and mumbled. I awoke to a tingling arm as the first light of day brightened the sky. My attempt to slip to the bathroom without waking Jill was unsuccessful as her eyes popped open when I swapped a pillow for my shoulder under her head.

"What time is it?"

I checked the alarm clock as I passed the nightstand. "Six. Go back to sleep."

She sat up in bed and stared out over the ocean. "I slept for nine hours."

Leaving the bathroom door open as I stripped for the shower, I replied, "You needed it. I don't think you've slept more than five hours a night since we went to Belize."

After showering, I pulled the curtain back and was surprised to find Jill leaning against the doorframe, wearing a loose cotton beach coverup bought in Naples. "Let's walk the beach before it gets busy."

I wiped myself with a towel. "You want to beat the kids to the sand dollars that washed up overnight?"

She handed me my swimsuit. A pair of sandals dangled from her other hand. "No, it's just…so peaceful in the morning. It's like having our own private beach."

I slipped on my swimsuit and the sandals. "Aren't you going to change?"

"I'm wearing my swimsuit under the beach coverup."

I smiled, thinking about our search for swimsuits…

I'd gone to the one rack of men's beachwear, found my waist size, then chose a suit I thought was nice. Jill had disappeared into a changing room with an armload of swimsuits. She'd popped out to check several in the mirrors, then went back in the changing room for another half hour. I assumed she'd chosen something when she emerged the next time, but she went back to the swimsuit display and pulled another two or three one-piece suits off the rack.

"Why don't you try on a bikini?" I'd asked.

Her withering glare reinforced my supposition that she wasn't comfortable exposing that much skin around strangers. "Women my age don't wear bikinis."

I retreated to a corner and looked through books identifying Gulf Coast seashells and fish. A young man with sun-bleached hair approached with a smile. "Can I help you, sir?"

"My wife is trying on bathing suits."

He gave me a knowing smile. "There's a comfortable chair next to the cash register, and this morning's newspaper is on the counter. Would you like a cup of Starbucks? We keep an urn in the backroom for our customers."

I laughed. "This is not an aberration?"

He shook his head. "It's a woman thing. Finding the right suit that accentuates the right attributes and hides the others is a trial. How do you take your coffee?"

I'd finished two cups before Jill eventually found an acceptable swimsuit. She didn't model it in the store. We walked back to the hotel where she'd put it on in our bathroom and emerged with it hidden entirely under the beach coverup.

"Don't I get to see the swimsuit?"

She pondered the question for a moment, then lifted the beach cover. The one-piece suit was spartan, blue with a rainbow of narrow diagonal stripes. The suit was without frills, skirt, or enhancements and made her look trim and girlish. She looked at me apprehensively, like she expected a negative comment.

"It's lovely and clings in all the right places."

She pulled the beach coverup down and squirmed. "I feel like I'm naked in it."

I knew there was nothing I could say, so I smiled and blurted out the one thing that came to mind, hopeful that it wouldn't start an argument, "That's not a bad thing."

We walked the Sanibel beach for nearly a mile before encountering another beachcomber. Jill became brave as the sun warmed the sand. She pulled off her coverup and handed it to me before wading into the surf, letting the swells swirl around her legs. After a few minutes, she walked back to me and strapped on her sandals and then strode with confidence past a group of teens rolling out blankets on the sand. The boys wore long, baggy surfer swimsuits, and the girls were in bikinis with thong bottoms. One of them opened a cooler and handed beer to the others.

When we were past the teens, I put my arm around Jill's waist and pulled her close. "You look better in your swimsuit than any of those youngsters."

Jill grinned. "Liar."

I ran my hand over her hip. "Seriously."

I remembered a sign warning that bathing suits and bare feet were prohibited in the dining area, so we rinsed the sand off our feet and went up to our hotel room to change into clothing appropriate for breakfast in the restaurant.

While Jill was in the shower, I changed and was about to slip my cell phone into my pocket when I noticed the voicemail icon blinking. The message from Matt, my National Park Service (NPS) boss, was succinct. "Call me."

I hit his number on the speed dial as I heard Jill singing a song I didn't recognize.

"What's up, Matt?"

"Really, Doug. Don't you ever have your phone on?"

"We're on vacation and are walking on the beach. What's up?"

"I hate to interrupt your vacation, but I have a request for your assistance with an investigation."

"Where?"

"Big Cypress National Preserve."

"Where's that, Louisiana?"

"It's in South Central Florida on the northern edge of the Everglades. A new portion of the preserve has been opened for oil and gas exploration. Several environmental groups have been fighting it in the courts, but the last appeal was overruled, and the drilling leases have been auctioned off. The oil drillers hired survey crews to mark the boundaries of the leases, and one of the survey crews is missing."

I heard the shower water stop, and Jill's singing became humming. I thought about how long it had taken her to overcome the trauma from our last case, how this was the first morning there had been happy singing in the shower.

"Matt, we're burned out, and Jill is having nightmares after our confrontation in Belize. I think we need to beg off this case while she recuperates."

Matt was quiet for so long that I thought he'd hung up. "Doug, this is a *big deal*. This request came from high up the chain of command. The regional superintendent said his boss wanted 'the A Team' assigned to this, not some wannabe law enforcement rangers fresh out of training."

"But…"

"You and Jill have friends in high places. In case you need to call in an IOU sometime, it'd be best if you didn't irritate them."

"Shit," I said as Jill walked out of the bathroom.

"Who are you talking to?" she asked, drying her hair.

I handed her the phone. "It's Matt." I walked into the bathroom and closed the door.

\* \* \*

"What did you find out from Matt?" I asked as we rode the elevator to the lobby.

"That he told you a survey crew is missing. There's been friction between environmental groups and the oil companies, and likely that's what's involved."

We went through the breakfast bar, got coffee, and found a table barely large enough for our plates and coffee mugs. Jill watched me butter a waffle as she spooned yogurt over granola.

"What?" I asked as I poured syrup over the waffle, scrambled eggs, and sausage.

"You'll burn through those calories in two hours and be ready to eat again."

I put a bite of waffle into my mouth. "Your point is?"

She shook her head, having given up on modifying my high-fat, low-fiber diet. "Matt said there's been vandalism at a couple of the drill sites, but no personal attacks. Surveyors have never become targets before."

"It's a mistake to theorize before you have data. If you do that, you twist the facts to fit your theories instead of the facts driving your theories."

Jill set down her spoon and looked at me. "Where did that come from?"

"We shouldn't assume the disappearance of the surveyors has anything to do with the oil drilling until we have solid information. They could be lost, or there are many other possible reasons they are missing."

She waved her spoon. "No, where did you come up with that profound statement?"

"You don't think I'm capable of a profound thought?"

"Spill it. Where did you pick up that line?"

"Sir Arthur Conan Doyle."

Jill resumed eating. "That makes more sense. It sounds more like Sherlock Holmes than Doug Fletcher."

"It's true. Don't assume anything until you've got facts to drive your theory."

Jill scooped up the last of the granola mixture and pushed the bowl aside. "Do you have any other profound quotes?"

"Never wrestle with a pig; you get dirty, and the pig enjoys it."

"That's a little less profound."

I mopped up the remaining syrup. "What inspirational quotes do you remember?"

"Mark Twain said, 'I didn't have time to write a short letter.'"

"I don't get it."

Jill leaned over, dropping her plastic bowl and spoon into a trash can. "I've read way too many rambling reports. If the writer had spent a few minutes gathering his thoughts before starting to write, I might've remembered the point he was trying to convey."

I got up and put my breakfast trash in the can. "I guess I'll let you write all our reports from now on."

Jill jumped up. "That wasn't the point I was trying to make."

Putting my arm around her waist, I pulled her close. "Too late, dear."

We packed our bags, checked out of the hotel, and drove south, roughly following the coastline. South of Naples, Jill directed me to the Tamiami Trail.

As I made the turn, Jill said, "There's the sign for Big Cypress National Preserve."

The developed areas of Naples and the coastal regions gave way to "old" Florida. The view changed to cypress swamp with an occasional pocket of development on a high spot. I pulled into Joanie's Blue Crab Shack when we reached Ochopee.

"Really?" Jill asked. "You ate a huge breakfast two hours ago."

"Look at the map and tell me where the next restaurant is."

Jill consulted a map on her phone and moved the view around with her fingertips. Without comment, she shut down the phone and jammed it in her pocket without admitting I was right. "I hope I can get a seafood salad."

Still in the car, I punched in the park headquarters number Matt had given me. During a very short conversation, the car went from cool to sweltering. I ended the call. "The superintendent and his law enforcement ranger are going to meet us here as soon as they can get free."

An eclectic mix of rental cars, battered pickups, motorcycles, and cars well past their prime filled the restaurant parking lot. The only vehicle out of place was the Florida State Trooper's car backed into the furthest corner of the lot.

The aroma of frying seafood permeated the small parking lot as we walked toward the building. Inside, a blackboard message: "*If you want fast food, keep trucking 42 miles west or 66 miles east, happy trails y'all,*" greeted us. Antlers, alligator skulls, hog tusks, and a diamondback rattlesnake skin, along with numerous red and blue ribbons, decorated the walls. The café was crowded, even before eleven o'clock, and I didn't see an open table. As I scanned the room, the trooper met my gaze and nodded to open chairs at his back corner table.

"We've been invited to join the trooper." Jill looked surprised but followed me through the maze of tables to the corner.

The trooper stood and pulled out a chair for Jill. "Ma'am, I don't see many women in law enforcement around these parts." He pushed the chair in for Jill and nodded to me as we sat.

Our host's hair was trimmed short and had a bit of gray at the temples. His jaw was square, and his uniform looked like he'd pressed it just before we arrived. In front of him was a plate with the remnants of egg yolk and toast crumbs, along with a partial cup of coffee. He reached out his hand. "Hal Rude."

After introductions, Jill studied the trooper's face. "How did you know we were cops?"

The corner of his mouth hinted at a smile. "Ma'am, cops look the same everywhere. And that badge on your belt and the Glock at your hip is a little obvious. What agency are you with?"

"The U.S. National Park Service."

The trooper raised his eyebrows. "Khaki shorts and golf shirts are a bit out of uniform."

"We're investigators. We usually wear civvies."

The trooper caught the waitress's eye, and he held up his coffee cup. "I hope you're not in a rush to get somewhere because the pace of life here is a little slower than in Miami." (He pronounced it My-ah-mah). "The food is cooked to order with loving care, and the cook doesn't run around like a teenager in a fast-food joint."

Jill smiled. "I kind of like this pace."

Hal shook his head. "Naw, it'll drive you Yankees crazy in about a week. You're used to talking, eating, and moving way too fast."

I looked around at the crowd. "I take it you're on call here."

"This is about as close to the middle of the Tamiami Trail as you can get and still find a cup of coffee. Later, I'll go out and ticket some idiots trying to set a land speed record between Naples and Miami, but most mornings, it makes more sense to stretch my legs and eat here where I can respond to a call from either direction."

The waitress brought ceramic mugs and menus for Jill and me, then poured coffee. "The cook's still doing breakfast, but the oil's hot, so we can also do anything on the lunch menu."

Jill looked up. "We're waiting for the superintendent from Big Cypress. We'll order after he arrives."

The waitress nodded. "The superintendent and the ranger called in their orders. If you choose something now, it'll be up about the time they arrive." She paused and leaned close. "The lima bean stew is our specialty, and it'll be ready in a few minutes."

I set my menu aside. "What's in the stew besides lima beans?"

The waitress looked surprised, like no one had ever asked before. "Uh, whatever the cook puts in. It's not like the recipe is written down."

The trooper leaned back with a smile on his face. "Don't worry, whatever's in it is wholesome and tasty."

Jill looked worried. "Alligator?"

The waitress nodded. "Most days."

Jill was about to delve further into the ingredients when I stopped her. "We'll both have the stew." I handed the waitress our menus, and she hustled away.

"I don't particularly want to sample possum, frog legs, or..." she looked at the snakeskin on the wall, "whatever that was."

Hal grinned from ear to ear. "That was a roadkill snake. It's not in the stew. More likely that there's some crabmeat, grouper, and maybe gator. Like I said, it's all wholesome and nutritious."

Jill wasn't pleased but didn't complain. She made sure no one was listening over the din of voices and leaned close to Hal. "What do you know about the missing surveyors?"

"I know they were staking out drilling leases and that they're missing. That's about it."

"Is there any chance their disappearance is an accident?"

Hal considered Jill's question. "Well, there's always a chance that it was an accident. I mean, cars go off the road all the time. I s'pose they might've veered off into swamp water in a ditch. Unless someone sees them go off, or unless I notice tread marks leaving the road, they might be drowned inside their truck, and no one would know."

Jill looked surprised. "Does that happen?"

Hal nodded.

"Often?"

"I think Yogi Berra said something profound like, 'you don't know what you don't know.' If a car disappears and the water level doesn't go down in the winter, who knows how many cars and trucks are in there."

I sighed. "I suppose people are reported missing, but 'you don't know what you don't know.'"

Hal nodded. "Too many people are missing, especially hookers, Miccosukee women, young drunk women, and runaways."

Jill closed her eyes. "Women."

Hal nodded. "More women than men, and more who are down on their luck than the party girls from South Beach." He looked up, then stood. "Your party of two just arrived. I'll clear out, and there'll be room for all of you."

Hal donned his trooper hat and met the two uniformed rangers halfway across the room. They shook hands, and Hal directed them to our table.

Conversations around us stopped as the two NPS rangers in full uniform threaded their way through the tables to our back corner. Jill and I stood. A woman seated behind Jill whispered to her tablemates when she noticed Jill's pistol and the badge on her belt.

The red-haired superintendent, his face ruddy from too many days in the sun, reached out his hand. "You must be the Fletchers. I'm Chad Campbell, and Cedric Washington is my law enforcement ranger."

Cedric's caramel-colored skin, black hair, and facial features were similar to a group of Miccosukee men sitting at the counter. He removed his Smokey Bear hat and smiled as he shook Jill's hand. "It's a pleasure to meet you, ma'am." His southern accent was thick, and he spoke with the slow, lilting cadence of the locals around us. He shook my hand. "Please call me Hawk. Only Chad and my mother call me Cedric."

The waitress arrived at our table with two cups and fresh coffee before Chad and Hawk were seated. "Your stew will be up in a second," she said as she cleared the remnants of the trooper's breakfast and wiped the table.

Hawk leaned close to Jill and whispered something that made her smile. Chad hung his hat on a peg and waited for the waitress to retreat before taking a seat. "I understand you've been sent to help with Hawk's investigation." He paused, then added, "I hope you're not wasting your time."

The comment surprised me. "Why would we be wasting our time?"

Chad looked at Hawk, whose face revealed no emotion. "People disappear here. It's the nature of the Everglades. We sometimes locate them or recover their remains. Other times, they're just gone without explanation."

Jill wrapped her hands around the coffee cup. "Which is the case here?"

Hawk leaned his arms on the table. "It's too early to tell, ma'am."

Jill met Hawk's eyes. "If we're working together, you'll call me Jill. If we're annoying you and unwelcome, you can continue to call me ma'am, and I'll call you Cedric."

Chad was ready to apologize, but Jill raised her hand, waiting for Hawk's response. "Ma'am is a southern term of respect for someone you don't know well."

"My Texas friend, Mandy, says ma'am is a condescending term she uses when she's dealing with an airhead she doesn't really want to know."

Hawk sipped his coffee to hide his grin. "Your friend sounds like a southern belle."

"Mandy is a perfect lady until you piss her off. Then she's a wildcat." Jill paused, "So, what's it going to be? Are we colleagues or are we intruding in your investigation?"

Hawk was smiling, but I could see Jill had touched a nerve. Chad stepped in. "Hawk's a good investigator, and he's only started looking into this case. I'm sure he welcomes your assistance, but you were assigned to help without us requesting assistance. To be honest, we don't know you or why you're here. Having two NPS investigators dropped in our laps is premature and a diversion from Hawk's investigation."

Hawk swirled his coffee. "If Chad hadn't dragged me here, I'd be out at the survey sites looking for tire tracks and other hints about what happened. Instead, here we are, drinking coffee and eating lunch."

On cue, our waitress arrived with a basket of homemade rolls, three steaming bowls of lima bean stew, and a plate that appeared to be covered with deep-fried chicken legs with a bowl of slaw on the side. Hawk was the only one who hadn't ordered stew, and he unfolded a napkin and spread it on his lap.

Jill observed his selection as he gnawed the meat off a bone. "That's not chicken."

Hawk shook his head and wiped his mouth until he finished chewing. "Joanie's got the best frog legs in the Everglades."

Jill looked at the half-dozen remaining legs. "Those frogs must've been huge."

Hawk picked up another frog leg and examined it. "These are medium-sized. We used to gig bigger ones when I was a kid."

I cut off Jill's question about *gigging* frogs and turned to Chad. "We're on vacation, and my superintendent asked us to meet with you. He's offering our assistance. If you don't want or need us, we'll gladly go back to the beach."

Chad and Hawk exchanged a glance but said nothing as I tasted a spoonful of my lunch. The stew had the consistency of a casserole, or Minnesota hotdish, and was bursting with flavor. A chewy bit of meat reminded me of tough chicken. Jill fished a bay leaf out of her stew, then stirred it.

Jill looked like she was waiting for it to cool off, but I was sure she was inspecting the contents. "This smells heavenly. I see ham and chicken bits."

Hawk finished off another frog leg before answering. "Joanie usually makes it with smoked ham hocks and gator." He paused and smiled. "But she sometimes slips in a surprise."

"Surprise?" Jill asked, still stirring the stew.

Hawk sensed Jill's reluctance to eat strange meats and decided to test her. "You might find a crawdad, a frog leg, or some possum, depending on what the cook can find."

Jill scooped up a spoonful, and a smile spread across her face as she chewed. "This reminds me of Mom's butterbean soup, only with seasonings she never used. It's wonderful!"

Hawk hid his disappointment by eating another frog leg. His attempt to ruin the Yankee woman's lunch had failed. Chad's expression told me there was something Hawk hadn't said.

"And?" I asked.

"There's no *and*," Hawk said.

I looked at Chad, who looked away and wiped his mouth.

"If we're partners in this, I want all the cards face-up on the table."

Chad was quiet for a moment, apparently considering his words. "I talked to the Everglades National Park superintendent just before we drove here. He told me you two pulled their butts out of a sling after his ranger dropped the ball on a death investigation. He sent me a couple of video links. You've investigated murders in Arizona, Wyoming, South Dakota, Minnesota, and Iowa."

Jill finished her stew and pushed the bowl away. "The death in Iowa wasn't a murder. It was an accidental fall."

Chad scraped the final tidbits of stew from his bowl with a homemade roll. "I read an article from the Rapid City newspaper, and it said Jill Fletcher pulled a Wyoming deputy sheriff off the highway and saved his life."

Jill nodded, and I glanced at Hawk, who appeared intrigued, hearing this background for the first time.

I took a breath and leaned close to Chad. "Please don't get the wrong idea from whatever you've read or heard. We're here to assist you, not take over your investigation. Tell us how we can help, and we'll do whatever we can."

A look passed between Chad and Hawk. Chad fingered his coffee mug. "It only takes one crazy protester to cross the line."

Sighing, Hawk closed his eyes. "I'm focusing on the eco-protesters, but we're afraid they may be a magnet for other fringe groups who thrive on chaos. We all remember the protests that got out of hand at the Capitol, in Minneapolis, and Seattle.

In each of those peaceful crowds were anarchists who used the main protest as a shield for their destructive activities."

"Do you believe the protesters are behind the surveyors' disappearance, Hawk?"

"I'm not ruling out that possibility."

Chad shook his head. "Honestly, I think the protesters are harmless."

"Someone isn't harmless if they're kidnapping survey crews," Jill said.

Chad shook his head again. "Let's not jump to conclusions. We don't know what happened to the surveyors. They might be lost in the swamp. If we hadn't received an order to meet you for lunch, Hawk might've found them by now."

"They disappeared two days ago. What did you discover yesterday?" I asked.

"I spent the day finding out where they'd been working. It took half the day for their office to call me back after they'd determined where the surveyors planned to work. The office person said they'd only left some chicken scratching on a notepad." Hawk popped the last bit of roll into his mouth and looked at Chad. "I'd like to take them out to the places the surveyors were working."

Chad nodded. "I apologize. I thought you two were bureaucrats sent to stir things up and second guess what we were doing." He drew a breath and let it out slowly, then looked at Jill. "You two are the real deal. I've never met a ranger who's fired her gun in the line of duty."

Hawk leaned back and nodded to Jill. "I'd be happy to have either of you back me up if I got in a pinch."

Jill smiled. "That's the biggest compliment you can give another cop."

Hawk's face displayed no emotion. "It is. I feel like I should address you as Investigator Fletcher."

"I'd prefer Jill."

Hawk leaned forward and put out his hand. "Jill it is."

I raised my eyebrows. "We're shaking hands again?"

Hawk reached across the table to me. "The first time, I was being courteous. Now, I'm welcoming you to the investigation."

Chad set his hands flat on the table, signaling the end of lunch. "So, we're happy to have you, and Hawk's ready to show you what he's got."

Hawk signaled for the waitress. "Not until we have a slice of key lime pie."

Chad jumped into the silence, attempting to be a good mediator. "Hawk's only scratched the surface of this investigation and asking for your help seems premature. You're welcome to join in, but we really don't know enough about what may have happened to be reaching out for assistance."

"What do you know so far?"

Hawk wiped his hands on a napkin after finishing the last frog leg. "The courts recently allowed oil and gas exploration to restart in Big Cypress National Preserve. Oil companies bid for leases, and surveyors are marking those lease boundaries. Drilling has begun on some of the high ground leases, but most leases are in swampy areas with poor access. The crew that disappeared was surveying one of those marginal areas."

"The drilling restarted? There was drilling before?"

Chad wiped his mouth. "There's a quirk in this park's ownership. The land was given to the federal government in the 1920s, but the family who donated the land retained the oil and gas rights. Drilling crews have been here since the 1930s, but it wasn't until the 1980s that anyone had the technology to separate the oil from the brine. They have to drill deep, over 11,000 feet, to reach the oil and gas deposits, then they have to separate the oil and inject the brine back into the aquifer. There was a drilling moratorium for a few years, but the courts upheld the legality of exploration and drilling. However, the oil companies can't use explosives to search for deep underground deposits. Companies bid on drilling claims, and now the surveyors are marking the boundaries of their leases."

Hawk nodded to the Miccosukee men at the counter. "The Miccosukee tribal council voted to allow drilling on the reservation. It's a nice source of revenue for the tribe, but even knowing how much money it's bringing in, some young tribal members have protested the drilling."

"I read an article about protesters." Jill said.

Hawk nodded. "Protesters are blocking access to the drilling sites, mostly peaceful tree huggers. They wave signs and shout at the trucks, but they're harmless."

# Chapter 3

Chad offered to drive our rental car to the park headquarters rather than leave it parked at Joanie's. I gave him the keys, and Jill and I got in the 4-wheel-drive NPS pickup with Hawk.

Jill rode in the front seat. "Hawk, tell us more about the oil drilling, surveying, and protesters."

"The family who owned the 700,000 acres of Everglades swamp knew about oil and gas under the preserve before donating the land to the Park Service. Like most government things, the opinion about whether to allow drilling or not swung like a pendulum with each change of the controlling party in Congress. During the '80s, the administration was cagey, allowing exploration and setting rules for drilling, but there was a holdup when it came time to auction the rights."

Jill frowned. "What kind of hold up?"

"Well, for a while, the environmental impact statement was reviewed by the courts, then the bidding process itself came under question. It seemed like every time things were lined up to start the process, an environmental group would get some bureaucrat's ear, and the drilling requirements changed. Then everyone would step back and start over."

"How did you feel about that?" Jill asked.

"Like most college kids, I believed it was wrong to drill at all, especially in a national preserve. Then I got the Park Service ranger job, and it irked me that road building was allowed through the swamp to bring in the drilling equipment, opening the risk of an oil spill that would contaminate the Everglades."

"And now?"

Hawk shrugged. "I've sworn an oath to uphold the laws and constitution of the United States. I'll defend whatever the courts allow." He paused and took a breath. "But sometimes it's hard to look at myself in the mirror and believe I'm doing the right thing by protecting the drilling companies."

"So, you're personally opposed to the drilling?"

"I am. But the drilling companies are careful, and they do site restoration after they leave a drilling pad. There's immediate damage to the vegetation, but in a couple years, no one can tell where they've drilled."

"How often do you see protesters?" Jill asked.

"They're out waving their signs nearly every day. There's some turnover, with several new faces on the weekends, but there's a nucleus of people who show up routinely. They're like Whack-a-Mole, moving from site to site, so there's no way to anticipate where they'll be next."

I leaned forward on the seatback. "Do you know who they are?"

"Yep, I've spoken with all of them, and I have names and addresses. They're from all over the country, but a nucleus group rented an old farmhouse, and they live in it like a commune."

"Tell us about the survey company."

"Actually, there are two companies, and they've divided the work up geographically. One company works out of Florida City, surveying eastern tracts, and a company out of Everglades City handles the west. The missing crew works out of Everglades City."

Hawk slowed as we approached a driveway crossing the waterway running alongside the road. "This is one of the survey sites I haven't checked yet." He activated the 4-wheel-drive and drove through gravel made from shells and ground coral, stopping when we reached a grassy area with two parallel crushed strips. He commented, "Someone's driven in here. Let's walk from here."

Leaving the truck, Hawk handed Jill a bottle of insect repellent.

Jill sprayed her arms, legs, and neck. "The superintendent from the St. Croix Scenic Riverway warned us that their mosquitoes were the size of Piper Cubs and would suck you dry in a few hours."

"The mosquitoes are smaller here, but they make up for their size by carrying nasty diseases."

Jill handed me the spray. "Mosquitoes up north carry West Nile virus and equine encephalitis."

Hawk laughed. "We have those, plus malaria, dengue fever, Zika virus, and a whole alphabet of other things I can't pronounce and don't want to think about."

After spraying my arms and face with bug repellent, I fell in step behind Hawk and Jill, inspecting the grass that tires had matted. "How far off the road do the surveyors go to mark out the drilling leases?"

"It varies. I think they were probably working a mile or so from here. There's a raised island, of sorts, that would support a drilling rig."

Jill glanced at Hawk. "Why are we walking if they were working a mile from here?"

"If you're walking, you see stuff on the ground. It's too easy to buzz past a bent grass stem or cigarette butt that might lead to something off the road when you're driving the pickup."

Jill turned her head and smiled at me. "It's a good thing I've had Doug walking the beach these past few days or he'd be wasted after a hundred yards."

Hawk nodded. "I'm used to walking along at my own pace. Let me know if you'd like me to slow down."

Jill stifled a laugh. "You might want to take it easy. Doug's pretty old to be boonie-bashing on foot. He patrols the Padre Island beach twice a day in a pickup."

"Texas is home for you two?"

"I'm originally from South Dakota, and Doug's from Minnesota. We're stationed on Padre Island National Seashore."

"After reading about your Devils Tower investigation, I'd guessed you two were stationed in Washington D.C."

"There are too many politicians in Washington. Doug and I prefer Texas. We may stay there after we retire."

Hawk glanced at me over his shoulder. "Since you're already making plans, is that date coming soon?"

Hawk assumed I was the one who would retire first. Jill was nearly five years older but worked out to stay trim. She dyed her naturally brown and gray hair at the urging of her friend, Mandy, an expert in all things feminine. Jill's workout routine and

Mandy's makeover left people assuming I was the older spouse.

"We've got a few more years, but we really like the Texas coast. Jill will inherit a South Dakota ranch some day, and she's hinted that the Black Hills might make a nice retirement location."

Hawk stopped abruptly, making me think he'd spotted something. He turned to Jill. "You seem like such nice sane people; why in hell would you move someplace where it snows?"

Jill laughed. "It's home."

Hawk shook his head. "But still, it snows!"

We resumed walking, and Jill asked, "Are you local?"

"I grew up on the Miccosukee reservation. We're only a few miles from where I was born. Other than college, I've never been out of the Everglades." Hawk paused, "The Black Hills are surrounded by reservation. You must've grown up with a lot of indigenous people."

"Not as many as you'd think. The Lakota have their own schools, so I didn't know many tribal members until college. The South Dakota universities are more of a melting pot than the schools in town."

"The entire Black Hills was originally part of a reservation."

Jill nodded. "It was reservation until gold was discovered."

Hawk nodded. "You know and understand the history."

"I do. The Miccosukee reservation is intact, isn't it?"

Hawk glanced at Jill, then back at me. "There wasn't anything of value to the Whites, so yes, it's intact. The oil and gas discoveries put some pressure on the tribe to allow drilling, but the courts have upheld the treaties, and so far, the reservation boundaries seem to remain safe. The water under the reservation is a different matter."

"What's going on with the water?" I asked.

"Well, the Everglades sits on top of a huge aquifer shared by the entire southern half of the state. It's either being drained, dammed, or polluted, depending on which area and decade you look at."

"And now?" I asked.

"You've read about the red tides on the Gulf coast? Well, there's a theory that those are caused by fertilizer leaching through the aquifer."

"I heard they're caused by global warming," I said from the back.

Jill sensed something Hawk hadn't said. "What do you think?"

Hawk shrugged. "It's convenient to blame the farmers or fossil fuels, but our Miccosukee oral history says there were red tides before the Spaniards arrived. It's hard to say modern fertilizer is the culprit when Ponce de León made reference to a red tide in his Gulf coast exploration during the 1500s."

Jill nodded. "But they're more frequent now."

Hawk shrugged. "Are they? Maybe, or maybe not. My ancestors didn't record frequency, just the occurrence. Huge die-offs of fish and birds have been happening for hundreds or thousands of years. Our lifetimes are the blink of an eye, yet we measure history in months, years, or decades. Mother Earth is very old, and we don't know what happened before records were kept. The whole state of Florida is quartz sand eroded from the Appalachian Mountains deposited on top of limestone and coral."

"The ecologists predict global warming will raise the sea levels and threaten the shoreline."

Hawk shrugged. "Ecologists think short-term. The geologists think long-term, and they've determined Florida was three times its current area during the last ice age. Since the glaciers covered Doug's home in Minnesota, the sea has risen for thousands of years. Where we're standing was once high savannah with grazing animals and sabre-toothed cats. The coastline was hundreds of miles west of here."

Hawk stopped. "I think the surveyors may have been back here. Tourists don't venture far off the roads, and I see truck tire tracks in the mud."

Jill looked at the imprint in the mud. Hawk took out his phone and photographed the tread pattern. "Can you tell if they're still back here, or did they leave?"

Hawk put his camera in his pocket. "The grass is bent toward the highway. Whoever entered left that way."

"Then, why are we walking farther back?"

Hawk smiled. "Because I want to know what they did when they were here."

We walked another fifteen minutes before Hawk stopped us again. "I see a survey marker ahead."

Fifty meters farther down the narrow road, we arrived at an opening with grass packed down and tire tracks cutting back and forth. Orange tape was attached to a wooden stake near the road. Other strips of orange ribbon fluttered from trees and bushes around us. Hawk stopped at the edge of the open area and studied it. "There's been more than one truck back here."

Jill looked at the glade. "Maybe they were here two days in a row."

Hawk squatted down and pointed to a muddy area. "Not unless they used different trucks each day. I see two different sets of tire treads." Hawk took out his phone and shot more photos of the muddy tracks.

I followed a set of tire tracks to a larger area of matted grass. "They must've unpacked their gear here." A splash of brown caught my eye, and I moved slowly ahead, hoping not to destroy the evidence. "There's blood splatter here."

Approaching me slowly, Hawk scanned as he walked. He squatted beside me, then took another few steps. "There's a pool of blood here."

Jill nudged me and pointed to our right. "There's another spray pattern there, but with white material, too."

I stood and took a deep breath. "Hawk, there's brain tissue splattered on the grass over here."

Hawk walked over and studied where Jill pointed. He drew a breath. "Someone didn't live through the trip back here."

I looked at Jill to judge her reaction. Her arms folded across her chest, and her eyes closed. "Are you okay?"

After a moment, she looked up and opened her eyes. She nodded toward the blood-stained grass. "I said a prayer."

Hawk nodded, agreeing that was an appropriate thing to do. "Not much else we can do for whoever that was." After photographing the blood splatter, Hawk donned a pair of neoprene gloves and placed samples from each spray pattern into evidence bags.

I tried to visualize the bullets' paths based on blood spray patterns and matted grass. "We should look for evidence. Let's walk a grid."

After twenty minutes of walking back and forth, shoulder to shoulder, we'd found two places where dirt had been disturbed by the impact of a bullet. Using a knife, Hawk gently dug the silver-colored bullets from the soft soil. He placed each into a plastic evidence bag, then handed one to me.

I held the bag up to inspect the projectile. "This looks like a cast lead bullet, and most factory loads are copper-clad or metal-jacketed."

Hawk examined the other bullet. "Some folks cast their own lead bullets and reload cartridges. Others are buying less powerful 'cowboy loads' for their old pistols. They're less likely to blow apart an antique rifle or revolver. I think those cartridges are loaded with lead-alloy bullets."

"Are we done?" Jill asked.

Hawk looked around the area we'd walked. "I'd like to get a metal detector and scan the area, but there's nothing we're going to accomplish right now." He paused and frowned. "Someone policed this area before they left. There's not a candy wrapper, cigarette butt, or used tissue."

Jill frowned. "Cigarette butt?"

"A lot of people around here still smoke. If there were three or four people here, odds are at least one of them was a smoker." Hawk glanced at the area we'd just searched. "There's not a filter or butt anywhere."

Walking back to the pickup, Hawk searched the east side of the road, Jill walked the middle, and I looked in the grass on the west. Hawk was an interesting character, and the more I was around him, the more I respected him as a cop.

"Water moccasin!" Hawk yelled, holding up his hand, signaling for us to stop. I pulled my pistol and retreated a step. Jill was frozen in the center of the road, searching the long grass, her hands in the air. Hawk looked back, then started to laugh. "I guess you two aren't snake people. He's gone."

I holstered my gun and walked toward Jill. "I don't like snakes, and I hate venomous snakes."

Jill relaxed but remained vigilant. "I've spent my childhood dodging South Dakota rattlers, then again as an adult in the Texas and Arizona desert. I have a deep respect for poisonous reptiles."

"The Everglades isn't a good place for you two. There are a thousand things here that'll bite you, sting you, or eat you."

Jill glared at him. "Thanks for those words of encouragement. You've made me feel so much better about being here."

Hawk shrugged and started back toward the truck. "I'm just telling you what we're up against. This region is a strange place, and many locals are as prickly as the biting animals."

Jill fell into step alongside him. "What do you mean about the people?"

"The locals have been here forever. My people, the Miccosukee, Seminoles, and other Native people, built the shell mounds being bulldozed for development. Some mounds are ten thousand years old. First came the Spaniards, looking for gold and the fountain of youth, then White fishermen, followed by ranchers and farmers. They've been here for generations and are even less accepting of new folks than the indigenous people. If you walk uninvited up someone's driveway, expect to be met with a shotgun."

"They're hostile?" Jill asked.

"Some are hostile, and others are just protecting their property. There's a lot of land out here and not many cops. We have meth labs in abandoned houses, meth heads, who steal to supply their habit, and just plain old bad folks who'd rather steal than work. There are the old-time locals, who don't dial 911 when they have a problem. They deal with it."

"Really?" Jill asked. "I grew up on a ranch, but we never ran anyone off that came to the door. If anything, Mom would invite them in for coffee and a sweet roll."

Hawk shook his head. "There's some southern charm here, but there are a lot of prickly folks that don't like strangers. I saw a sign next to one driveway that said *I don't dial 911. I shoot, shovel, and shut up.*"

"Yeah, I saw a few of those signs in the Black Hills," Jill conceded.

"What about the traffic on the Tamiami Trail?" I asked. "The locals have to be used to all the people driving through."

"What about it? There are lots of tourists and truckers highballing across the Everglades on their way someplace else. Most don't even slow down unless they're buying gas or stopping at Joanie's to eat before they drive on."

Nearing the truck, I stopped searching the roadside. "So, you think some of the people who disappear fall victim to locals who just deal with them and shut up?"

Hawk turned to me and put his hands on his hips. "I don't *know* that, but I suspect it."

Jill looked distressed. "Their cars or vehicles are found."

"There's some of that, but there are also hitchhikers at both ends of the trail looking for rides across. I suspect some of them never make it to the other side of Florida."

Jill let out a breath, "The missing women."

Hawk unlocked the truck and started the air conditioning while Jill and I stood by the open doors. "There's a rumor that some truckers only pick up hitchhikers in return for something. 'Gas, ass, or grass' is the line I hear."

Jill and I got in the pickup. Grimacing, Jill said, "I thought that was an urban legend."

Hawk backed the truck down the narrow berm until he found a place wide enough to turn around. "Urban legends have a thread of truth to them." He stopped during his turn and stared at Jill. "If I were you and afraid of getting stranded on the road, I'd make sure I had some gas money in my shoe."

Jill looked at me in the back seat, like she expected me to rebut Hawk's comments. I shook my head. "I've heard the gas, ass, or grass phrase. I think a young woman has to be pretty desperate or naïve to hitchhike in this day and age."

Hawk's face lost all expression. "It's not just young women who are the victims of hitchhiker crimes." He drove toward the highway.

Jill turned to Hawk. "Please stop for a second."

46

He braked, and Jill jumped out of the truck and paced behind the tailgate. Hawk looked at me. "Did I offend her with the gas, ass, or grass line?"

"I don't have a clue."

Jill got back in and buckled her seat belt.

I asked, "Are you okay?"

"Yeah, I'm fine now."

"Now? What was wrong?"

She flipped her hand. "It's okay."

Hawk looked at her curiously. "You're sure?"

"I'm fine. I had a little backdoor breeze from the lima bean soup."

I leaned on the seatback. "What are you talking about?"

"Mandy taught me that southern ladies occasionally have to step out to release their backdoor breeze."

I started laughing. "We stopped so you could fart?"

Jill colored. "That's an impolite term for it. But yes, I didn't want to stink up the truck."

Hawk laughed and pounded the steering wheel. "That's precious, a backdoor breeze. Who's this Mandy?"

"Mandy's her Texas best friend, a real-life debutante."

"I've met a few of them," Hawk said. "They've got perfect hair, makeup, and clothes. They wouldn't say shit if they stepped in a cow pie."

Jill shook her head and stared out the side window until we got to the highway. With the truck stopped, Hawk looked at her. "Do you need another backdoor breeze stop?"

"Just drive."

# Chapter 4

The National Park Service headquarters was in a visitor center on a loop off the Tamiami Trail. The two-story building looked like any other NPS structure with a few rental cars in front of the parking lot, and in the rear, a mixture of older cars and pickups undoubtedly owned by the staff. Hawk parked in the back under the shade of a cypress tree.

"Chad's office is here in the back," Hawk explained. "He's got a wall map showing the older capped wells, pumping wells, drill sites, and the new leases getting surveyed."

Jill took a few steps, then turned and walked away from us.

"More backdoor breezes?" I asked.

She flipped her hand without looking back. "I'll be there in a minute."

Hawk led me down the sidewalk toward the front of the building, stopping at a bronze plaque set in the ground. "I think it's nice that people walk past this tribute to Steven Mather. Most of them don't know that he was a driving force behind the formation of the national park system."

Reading the plaque, I was moved by the description. "*Mather laid the foundation for the National Park Service, defining and establishing the policies under which its areas shall be developed and preserved unimpaired for future generations. There will never come an end to the good he has done.*"

"That's pretty profound," I said.

Hawk nodded. "It's good there were people like him who had a vision. Too bad it's not part of the Miccosukee reservation."

"Where's the remaining reservation?"

"Part of the rez is a peninsula surrounded by the preserve, and the rest abuts the north edge."

Jill caught up with us in time to hear Hawk's comments. "The tribe isn't pleased?"

Hawk shrugged as he walked with us to the front door. "What's done is done. The elders are pleased the preserve stopped the 1920s development around us."

"Was that when the big development occurred here?" I asked.

"New York developers were selling 2 to 5-acre tracts of *prime Florida real estate*. Their investors had no idea where their chunk of land was or that their land was a swamp with no road access. Or that the same tract was resold to possibly two to ten other buyers. When the scheme collapsed, it left a patchwork of parcels with questionable titles. The bottom line, people moved here. The early ranchers thought they could let their cattle roam the Everglades like in the Old West before barbed wire fences. Eventually, they fenced their land, some started vegetable truck farms, and others attempted raising everything from citrus to mangoes and avocados."

"I assume most went bust?"

Hawk shrugged. "Some families are still around, some sold out, and some just pulled up stakes and moved away."

Jill paused inside the door. "And now there's oil and gas drilling."

Hawk nodded but didn't comment. "Bathrooms are on the left, and the stairway to Chad's office is to the right."

After a bathroom stop, I found Hawk and Jill standing beside a glass enclosure with a taxidermy mount of a cougar. "I thought Florida panthers were black."

Hawk smiled, and I sensed a lesson coming. "The Florida panthers, like this mount, are actually a subspecies of the cougar family in the Puma genus. Pumas, or cougars as they're sometimes called, are the only large cats that don't roar. They have a mewling sound and sometimes let out a scream that sounds eerily like a woman. The black panthers are in the genus Panthera and are a melanistic variety of the jaguar family. If you see one in bright daylight, their spotted coat is sometimes visible."

Jill smiled, apparently aware of the trivia I'd just learned. "Both species are very shy."

Hawk nodded. "Not many Whites are quiet and patient enough to see a big cat." He nodded toward the corner. "Let's go upstairs and talk to Chad about oil leases."

Chad was working at his computer when we walked into his small office. The window behind his desk looked out over a trail where park visitors watched alligators in the waterway. Chad shut down the screen and stood. "Did you find the surveyors?" His smile revealed he knew we hadn't. He gestured for us to be seated, and like a gentleman, he waited for Jill to sit before taking his seat.

I looked at Hawk, not wanting to steal his show. "We found blood at the last survey spot."

Chad sat up. "Are you sure it was human?"

I nodded. "We haven't tested it, but there was also tissue. And we found where a couple of bullets impacted the ground in an area where there'd been human activity."

Chad ran a hand over his face. "We have a murder?"

"It looks that way," I replied.

Chad sat up. "You found blood and tissue but no bodies?"

Jill nodded. "No bodies and no sign of their truck or equipment."

Chad closed his eyes and leaned back. "I'll fill out an incident report, and I need to implement a follow-up plan. What are your thoughts?"

I waited a beat for Hawk, not wanting to steal his investigation. When he turned to me, I offered my thoughts. "Hawk's got some bullets recovered at the site along with blood and tissue samples, and those need analysis at a crime lab. After that, I'd like to interview the protesters."

Chad's eyes narrowed. "They didn't strike me as violent."

"They're unhappy with the drilling. If nothing else, we need to eliminate them as suspects. Hawk says they're out here every day, so even if they're not the murderers, they might've seen something suspicious." With no one else offering comments, I went on. "We need to identify the missing surveyors and talk with their colleagues and families."

Chad frowned. "We've got the surveyors' names and addresses. I think the sheriff has already told the families they're missing."

"The surveyors' families are suspects too. More than half of all murderers are known to their victims. Spouses are at the top of that list, followed by jilted lovers."

Jill wrinkled her nose. "Most of those are killings in the heat of the moment. Someone drove out there and killed those people in the middle of nowhere. I don't see an angry spouse doing that."

"Killing your spouse miles from where you live and near a place where people are protesting the surveying and drilling is a perfect way to deflect suspicion from yourself."

Chad got up and closed the office door. "There's a wild card here. You've got to assume every vehicle has a gun in it. A drunk with a burr under his blanket and a gun is pretty unpredictable, right Hawk?"

"I've pulled over a few vehicles for speeding. Most of them are just tourists in a hurry, but once in a while, it's a local redneck. They're not pleased about being pulled over and less pleased when they see that I'm an Indian about to issue a citation."

"Really?" Jill asked with a wry smile. "You have prejudiced rednecks?"

Hawk turned to her. "It's a thing here, just like at your home in South Dakota. Some people are displeased there's a reservation, and they are even more unhappy that the government has this big tract of land. Feds, Indians, and strangers aren't well received. Keep that in mind if

54

your car breaks down and you walk up to a house to ask for help."

Jill shook her head. "If someone came to the ranch and told my father their car broke down, he'd put tools in his truck and go to help them."

"Don't get me wrong. There are some nice folks here who'd do just that but there are other places you'd likely get met at the door with a shotgun than a smile." Hawk nodded to Jill's badge. "I'd put your Park Service identification out of sight before I walked up to anyone's door."

"I'd think they'd be more concerned about my walking up with a gun."

"People sometimes carry pistols. That's part of the ranch culture. A federal cop badge is different. That goes back to prohibition when the G-men came around to bust the moonshiners." Chad paused. "And that's another thing. The moonshining didn't stop when prohibition ended. There are stills in the woods, and a moonshiner might shoot before asking questions. And your body won't be found."

I leaned back. "The news just keeps getting better and better."

Chad laughed. "My future mother-in-law took me aside when I started dating my wife. She said, 'I've got a shotgun, a shovel, and eighty acres. If I find out you've hurt my girl, they won't find your body.'"

Jill smiled and looked at me. "Isn't that what Daddy said to you before our wedding?"

"Something like that."

Chad looked at his watch. "Where are you staying tonight?"

Jill glanced at me, "We checked out of our beach hotel. There's got to be some places closer."

I saw Chad glance at Hawk, who smiled. "There aren't any nearby motels on the federal list of preferred properties. The nearest is a place in Ochopee, and they rent cottages."

Jill caught Hawk's smile. "And the nearest place approved by the travel office?"

"There are chain motels in Florida City, but it's more than an hour away."

"What's the other direction?"

"Everglades City is fifteen minutes west of us and has a couple motels, but they're not on the federal list either."

Jill couldn't stop staring at Hawk's smiling face. "What's the joke?"

"We don't get many VIPs, but when they visit, they stay in Miami or Naples."

"So, we're being tested. You want to see if we'll stay in a mom-and-pop place or if we'll drive more than an hour to stay in something more luxurious."

Hawk shrugged.

Jill kept her eyes on Hawk. "Tell me about the place in Ochopee."

"It's five minutes away; the cabins are rustic but clean."

"We won't have to shake cockroaches out of our shoes in the morning?"

Chad laughed. "This is Florida and checking your shoes in the morning is a good idea whether you're camping or staying in an upscale resort."

"Will you call the Ochopee place and see if they have any openings?"

Chad picked up the phone and dialed the number from memory. He made reservations, and said we'd be there shortly. He told them to charge the cottage to the park. "Your cottage awaits."

"You didn't have to look up the number," Jill said.

"My family stayed there last week."

I shook my head. "Did we pass the test? Are we just average folks?"

Hawk continued to smile. "Depends on how the night goes."

"Why?" Jill asked.

"Be careful not to step on a water moccasin when you go to the outhouse in the dark."

Jill didn't flinch. "I've got a flashlight, and I've used an outhouse before. I'm more concerned about a brown recluse spider hiding under the toilet seat."

Chad raised his hands. "Enough! The cottages have indoor plumbing."

Hawk continued smiling. "Most of them."

* * *

The cottages shared a check-in office with a campground. Less than five minutes from the visitor center, the setting had the feel of the Everglades. The parking lot was crushed shells, and the cottages were arrayed behind the office, each with a thatched roof.

Jill stopped short of the office. "I'm all into rustic, but I'm not sure I want to sleep in a building with a thatched roof."

Hawk held the door for us. "There are shingles under the thatch; they put the grass on top to make them look more rustic."

The woman behind the counter had a deeply lined face that made her look a hundred years old. Her smile was warm, and her voice pure southern honey. "Y'all must be the rangers." She froze for a second. "The park only reserved one cottage."

Jill smiled. "It's okay. We're married."

"I'll be. I've never had married rangers stay here." She made a point of leaning to the side to see Jill's Glock pistol. "I hardly ever see any ranger except Hawk wearing a pistol. You know how to use that thing, dear?"

"I've been carrying a gun since I was in high school."

"Well, bless you, dearie. You'll fit right in around here. We all carry big old guns."

I set my government credit card on the counter. "I assume you'll take a government credit card."

"Chad's got your cottage covered. But I hope you don't mind, though. The only cottage I've got left is the one with the hot tub on the porch." She pushed the credit card back. Sensing Jill's concern about the hot tub, she smiled. "You don't need to worry, dearie. All the cottages face the swamp, and you can get in and out of the hot tub without anyone seeing you but the gators."

Accepting our key attached to a hefty plastic tag, I picked up my suitcase. "Where do you recommend we go for supper?"

"Unless you plan to drive to Everglades City, your choice is Joanie's. I think she's got crawdads tonight."

We thanked her and walked out the door onto the gravel path. The cabin was more than rustic but neat and clean, as promised. Jill put her suitcase on the floor and flopped on the bed. "What do you think about the Big Cypress National Preserve?"

"I think this is a scary place."

"The rednecks or the critters?"

I set my suitcase on a stand. "Both." I dug to the bottom of the bag and pulled out a holstered snub-nosed revolver.

Jill sat up. "What's that?"

"It's my undercover pistol. I used to carry it in St. Paul when I did drug and prostitution busts. It doesn't scream 'cop' like the automatic pistols we carry."

Jill cocked her head. "Why get it out here?"

"The scout motto is 'Be prepared.'"

"The seven P's the South Dakota sheriff talked about before our Spearfish prostitution bust were, 'prior proper planning prevents piss poor performance.'"

"In this case, I can foresee situations where an extra gun would be wise."

"You'll need more firepower than your service pistol?"

I strapped the small holster to my ankle. "I'd rather have it and not need it..."

"...than need it and not have it," Jill said, completing my thought.

I laughed. "We've been married long enough for you to finish my sentences?"

"Only the cop adages." Jill got up. "I'm hungry. Let's find supper."

"If you'd eaten all your stew..."

"There were meat bits in there that worried me."

Our porch overlooked a swampy area. Jill stopped at the top step and pointed across the water. "I think that black thing is a gator."

I took her elbow and urged her down the steps. "Let's not hang around and find out."

"There's a fence, Doug."

"Do you really believe that flimsy thing is going to stop a hungry alligator?"

"He looks pretty content."

"Let sleeping gators lie."

Drawing a deep breath, Jill plodded ahead. "What are the chances Joanie has something besides crawdads tonight. I'd kind of like something green."

"I saw deep-fried okra on the menu."

"When I said green, I was thinking about a salad, not a deep-fried slimy pod."

I pushed the remote and unlocked the car doors. "When in Rome…"

"The Romans didn't eat deep-fried vegetables."

"Aha! You admit okra is a vegetable."

"Shut up and drive."

Joanie's Blue Crab Shack was a mile from the cottages. Jill stared out the window at the passing Everglades. "This is so desolate. The Everglades have their beauty, but there's water everywhere."

"Unlike Spearfish, where the ranchers fight over water rights."

"It seems so strange that people are fighting over the diversion or damming of water here when it's literally everywhere."

I parked, and we got in a short line at Joanie's. The blackboard choices had changed. As predicted, crawdads topped the menu. There were a dozen other choices, but everyone ahead of us ordered crawdads and hush puppies.

Staring at the blackboard, Jill stepped up to the counter. "Could I get a salad?"

Joanie, or the aged woman behind the counter I assumed to be Joanie, smiled. "Honey child, the kitchen would be delighted to whip up something. How about a seafood salad with shrimp, crab, and crawdads?"

"That sounds lovely. Do you have a vinaigrette dressing?"

"I have a homemade Italian."

"Wonderful," Jill said, stepping back so I could approach the counter.

"I'll have the crawdads and hush puppies special. And a cold long neck."

Joanie wrote my order down and looked at Jill. "Would you like something to drink? Maybe a sweet tea?"

I could almost hear Jill's inner self yelling, *"Nooo!"* She searched the blackboard for another option. "Unsweet tea?"

"Hot or cold?"

"Iced, please."

Joanie nodded. "I'll have Glory brew up a pot and ice it. Anything else?"

I glanced at Jill, and she smiled, knowing what was coming. "Two key lime pies."

The order for two surprised her. "I might not have room for pie. Just get a second fork so I can sample."

I looked at Joanie and wiggled my eyebrows. "Did I say either of them was for her?"

Joanie added the pie to our order. I paid cash and left a generous tip that made Joanie smile. "You were here with the cops at dinnertime."

Jill nodded. "We're working with the park rangers at Big Cypress Preserve."

A short line had formed behind us, but Joanie ignored them and leaned over the counter. "Be careful. Sometimes people disappear when they start poking around here. The local Bubbas tend to get their noses out of joint when strangers show up asking questions."

We took a corner table in the half-full restaurant. Jill sat on one of the chairs with her back to the wall, surveying the crowd.

"You used to sit with your back to the crowd."

"Your damned cop cynicism is rubbing off on me. I'm scared someone is going to walk up from behind and shoot me."

"I'm here to protect you."

Jill raised her eyebrows. "Like you protected me at the bar in Wisconsin? I think you'll recall I was entirely capable of looking out for myself."

"You blindsided that guy. He was focused on me and didn't see you as a threat."

"And I'd like to be in a position to see guys like that coming before they throw a punch at you."

"So, you're protecting me?"

Jill smiled and didn't answer, saved by the delivery of a giant salad covered with crawdad tails, shrimp, and lumps of crab meat. I got a platter of crawdads and hush puppies, with sides of coleslaw, drawn butter, and cocktail sauce.

Jill surveyed her salad with awe. "I'm not going to have room for even a bite of your two slices of pie." She paused. "Would you like my crawdads?"

"Try them."

Jill drew a breath and reluctantly speared one of the pink morsels, the size of her pinkie finger. She tentatively bit off a piece the size of a lima bean and chewed. Her eyes lit up, and the rest of the crawdad followed the first tentative bite. "The flavor is halfway between shrimp and lobster. They're wonderful."

I dipped a crawdad in cocktail sauce and popped it into my mouth. "See, I thought you'd like them."

The words were barely out of my mouth when the fire hit me. I took a long drink from my beer as Jill watched, curious about what was happening. "What's the matter?"

"I've never had cocktail sauce with this much horseradish." The vapors rose into my sinuses, and my eyes started to water.

"Maybe you should dip one in butter. Dairy kills hot pepper burning."

"Horseradish burn isn't from capsaicin, so I'm not sure dairy will work."

Jill was eating her salad and grinning ear to ear. "Is the beer helping?"

"No."

"Then, try the butter."

The butter helped, and so did a hush puppy, but maybe just through dilution. "The cocktail sauce is wonderful, but maybe in smaller portions."

I was full after my dinner, and Jill was only two-thirds of the way through her salad when Joanie delivered the pie. She sat down in a spare chair and smiled. "Everything to your liking?"

Jill wiped her mouth. "The salad is wonderful. Thanks for whipping up something special."

Joanie waved off Jill's thanks. "We don't get much call for salads, but we can make one anytime. How were the crawdads and hush puppies?"

I pushed the plate aside and pulled a slice of pie toward me. "It was all good. Thanks."

Joanie waited for me to take a bite of pie, then she leaned forward. "Y'all looking into those survey people who disappeared?"

Jill looked around the nearby tables. Seeing no one paying attention to us, she replied, "Yes, we're here to help Hawk investigate."

Joanie nodded. "Like I said before, y'all be careful. The locals have their undies in a bunch about all the strangers roaming around with survey and drilling equipment. Don't wander off alone—and watch your backsides."

"Is there something or someone special that makes you say that?"

"I hear things. You two are Yankees and feds. The locals don't take kindly to that combination." Joanie reached out and placed her hand on Jill's. "You're welcome and safe here but be careful where you step when you get off the highway."

Jill looked uneasy. "We're staying at the cottages up the road."

"You'll be fine there. Jubal keeps a shotgun under the counter. Ain't no one going to bother his customers."

Joanie left, and Jill slid a piece of pie in front of her. She forked off a bit and slipped it into her mouth, savoring it for a moment with her eyes closed. Then her eyes popped open as her gaze settled on me.

"Earlier you said you didn't feel comfortable here. Did you sense something I didn't?"

"I watched the people when we ate lunch. Only the tourists smiled at us or nodded. The locals looked away when they saw our badges."

Jill took another bite of pie and appeared thoughtful. "Everyone smiled and nodded to us when we walked into the Black Hills restaurants."

"And most folks were happy to talk to us. I don't think that'll be the response we get here."

We finished the pie and walked out. Not one local looked up as we passed tables. Jill scanned the parking lot as we walked to the car. "I don't like looking over my shoulder all the time."

I started the car. "Welcome to law enforcement."

"I thought it was because of the locals?"

"There's a predator in every crowd regardless of where you are. You have to watch people's eyes everywhere. Be very watchful of people who glance at you and make a point of looking away, or who hold you in a stare like they're challenging you."

Jill buckled her seat belt and sighed. "I used to think you were jaded and cynical. Now, I'm starting to think you're just vigilant."

# Chapter 5

The sun shined into the rearview mirror as we drove back to the campground and cottages. I locked the car and surprised Jill by suggesting we walk to the office rather than directly to our cottage. A bell tinkled when I opened the office door, and a large man wearing western-cut clothes came out of the backroom smiling. His hair was sun-bleached, and his skin was lined and deeply tanned. White pockmarks on his face hinted at an ongoing battle with skin cancer from years of working outdoors.

"Can I help y'all?"

"I think your wife checked us in a while ago."

The man studied us for a second before responding. "Sure, you're the rangers in cottage three, Fletchers. Is there a problem?"

I shook my head. "No problem. We ate at Joanie's and several of the locals didn't seem happy to see us, and I'm concerned some of them might come by later."

Extending his hand, the man introduced himself. "Jubal Foster. I believe you're Doug and Jill, right?"

We shook hands. "Right. We're here helping with an investigation."

Jubal nodded. "I heard some surveyors went missing."

"We've heard some rumblings that local folks aren't happy with us nosing around."

Jubal ran his hand over his bald scalp. "The locals don't like anyone snooping around. Between eminent domain seizures, the preserve, moonshining, ranch foreclosures, and generally being ornery, they've got a general mistrust of anyone wearing a badge."

"Are we a problem for you?"

Jubal smiled. "You're no problem for me. There's only one driveway in, and the swamp surrounds the whole campground. The locals know I keep a double-barrel shotgun under the counter. One barrel is rock salt. If someone doesn't get the hint to leave with a load of salt in their butt, the other barrel is buckshot." Jubal paused to make sure I got his meaning. "You're safer here than in a Miami hotel."

"I appreciate that. Thanks."

I turned to leave, but Jubal hadn't finished. "I hear Mizz Fletcher is pretty good with a gun. If you hear a second shot, I'd be happy to have Jill keep an eye out while I reload."

Jill got a Mona Lisa smile. "Who told you that?"

"I took the follow-up call from Chad after you checked in. The video of your Wyoming news conference impressed him."

"I'm never far from my Glock."

"You two go get a good night's rest. Things will be fine." He paused. "You've got a hot tub on your porch. Sit in it and relax. It'll make you fall asleep easier. No one can see your porch, so you can make up your mind if you want to wear a bathing suit or not."

We walked to the cottage on the crushed shell trail. Jill sidled next to me and took my hand. "I think we should hop in the hot tub for a while."

"Are you trying to seduce me?"

"I'm hoping to relax and forget my paranoia about local yokels sneaking up behind me."

Squeezing her hand, I said, "I might be able to distract you."

"Your mom called and asked me to make sure you're getting enough fiber. She heard you only eat hamburgers, and she's afraid you'll get a blockage."

I stopped. "You certainly know how to kill the mood. Mentioning my mother and her concerns about my bowel health in the same sentence..."

Jill smiled, her dimples showing. "Gotcha." She let go of my hand and raced to the cottage like a kid running away after teasing her friends.

She walked out of the bathroom dressed in her new swimsuit just as I closed the bedroom door. "You're really going to wear your swimsuit in the hot tub?"

"Yes, and so are you."

Stripping off my pants, I said, "I'm planning to go au natural."

"No, you're not. You'll get ideas."

"I already have ideas. According to Cosmopolitan, men think about sex once a minute."

Digging in my suitcase, Jill pulled out my swim trunks. "When did you start reading Cosmo?"

"I saw the headlines next to the cash register in the grocery store."

Laying my bathing suit on the bed, Jill leaned on the doorframe. She crossed her arms. "And what do women think about once a minute?"

"I don't know. The cashier would've made me buy the magazine if I'd opened it up to read the article."

"Ahh, you don't care enough about women's thoughts to spend four bucks on a magazine."

I froze, knowing once again the taste in my mouth was my foot. "You know that's not what I meant. I..."

"Doug."

"What?"

"When you're at the bottom of the hole, stop digging."

Sighing, I put on the swimsuit. "The chlorine in the hot tub is going to fade the swimsuits."

"I'll just have to buy another."

"I sat in the store for an hour while you tried on..."

"You're digging again." Jill cut me off. "And if you say yes, dear," she paused, "you'll be sleeping on the couch with a cracked rib."

I kissed her on the cheek. "As usual, you're right."

She marched through the living room and onto the porch. "I hope the couch cushions aren't lumpy."

I slid into the hot tub and took a deep breath. The water jets pulsated against the knots in my shoulders, and I felt the muscles relaxing. With my eyes closed, I was falling asleep when I felt Jill's toe run up the inside of my thigh. "I thought I was sleeping on the couch."

"I may forgive you if you fulfill your husbandly duty."

"My husbandly duty?"

The water swirled as Jill stood up. "I'll shower to rinse off the chlorine and meet you in bed."

\* \* \*

Something woke me, and I reached for my pistol on the nightstand. Lying still, I tried to process what I'd heard but could only recall the sound not fitting with whatever I'd been dreaming. Moonlight cast a dim glow through the window blinds, providing enough light to see the outlines of the room furnishings. The swamp had unfamiliar noises, but it provided a constant background of insects and frogs, and those weren't what I'd heard.

"What's up?" Jill asked, reacting to my quick motion to grab the gun.

"Shh."

I felt her shift in bed as she reached for the Glock pistol on her nightstand. A moment later, the deep bass call of a giant bullfrog echoed in the swamp, the point of origin near our cottage. The red numerals on the clock showed 3:57.

"Was that what woke you?"

"We don't want to be lying here if someone comes through the door with a gun," I whispered, easing out of bed. I slowly walked to the wall and peeked out the window. The moon was nearly full, the area around the cottage lit like daylight, and nothing was moving.

Jill made a series of scraping noises.

"What are you doing?" I hissed.

"I'm putting on clothes."

"Clothes are not a priority right now."

"I'm naked, dammit. I'm putting on underwear."

"Can you do it quietly with the Glock in your hand?"

"No, I can't."

I couldn't believe it. We were arguing about underwear when there might be someone intent on killing us just outside the cottage. "Underwear is not a priority right now. Check your side of the cottage."

"Not without panties and a bra."

"If someone is here to shoot us, they won't care if you're naked or dressed."

"I care. What if my mother has to identify me in the morgue?"

"They cover your body with a sheet."

"No, they don't! I've been to autopsies with you, and the person is naked."

I clenched my eyes shut. "They cut the clothing off the bodies."

"The first question my mother would ask is, 'Did she die wearing clean underwear?'"

I gave up on stealth. If there were anyone outside listening, we'd have heard them laughing. "Just look out your window and tell me if you see someone sneaking around."

"Hang on. I'm fastening my bra."

"If there's someone out there…"

"I don't want to be standing here without at least my bra and panties on."

A deep sound, halfway between a dog growl and someone burping after drinking a beer, echoed in the swamp. "That was the sound that woke me."

Jill sighed. "I think that was a gator roaring."

"They roar?"

"It's called a roar."

I looked out the door, then returned to bed.

"What are you doing?" Jill asked.

"I'm going back to sleep."

"Like hell you are. You roust me out of bed, get my adrenaline pumping, argue with me about confronting an unknown intruder without clothes on, and then you're going back to bed?"

"It's only four in the morning. Go back to sleep for a couple more hours."

The blue glow of the television lit the room as someone touted the virtues of an incredible kitchen knife that could cut a nail and still slice a ripe tomato. "You're going to watch infomercials while I sleep?"

"No."

"That's what it sounds like."

"You're not going to sleep."

"Why not?"

"I already told you, I'm too wound up to sleep. Entertain me."

I reached across the bed and put my hand on her flat stomach.

"Stop that! We're not fooling around again this morning."

Sliding my hand toward her navel, I purred. "You used to like me waking you up like this."

She grabbed my middle finger and bent it back. "Stop there, or you'll need a splint for a broken finger."

"I..."

"You woke me up and scared me half to death, then argued about whether I should confront an armed intruder naked or in my underwear. That got you no points. None. As a matter of fact, it cost you points. You're running an amorous deficit, and it may be weeks before I'll be willing to even discuss the possibility of romance."

My laughter cost me an elbow to the ribs. "Ow!"

"Serves you right."

"Would you rather I let you sleep until I was sure someone was sneaking up on us?"

"Yes. Well, maybe." Jill drew a breath. "No, but don't EVER expect me to confront an intruder naked. Never. Are we clear on that?"

"You usually wear a flannel nightgown that drags on the floor."

"Well, I was hot after we..."

Sitting up, I turned on the lamp. "See if there's something other than infomercials on the television."

"I kind of like the knife set."

My glare met a smile from Jill. "What time do you think Joanie starts serving breakfast?"

"Take a shower, and I'll make two cups of coffee in the toy coffee machine."

I flipped through the channels and found a 24-hour news channel, then made coffee. My cell phone said Joanie opened at 11:00, apparently catering to the lunch crowd. I found a café ten minutes farther west that opened earlier and had great breakfast reviews.

Jill was sipping coffee, fluffing her hair, and watching the news when I walked out of the bathroom. "It looks like another hurricane is headed for the Yucatan Peninsula, they predict it might cross over and sweep up the Gulf toward Texas." She watched me slip on underwear and pants. "How can you do that?"

"Do what?"

"Stand there naked in front of the windows?"

"There's no one outside."

"Still…"

"Being in sports locker rooms and Army basic training made me oblivious to being naked around other guys."

"We're not in a locker room. We're in a rental cottage, and you're standing in front of an open window."

I pulled on a shirt and buttoned it. "You're not talking about me getting dressed in front of a window. You're talking about me being naked in front of you. We're married, and we've seen each other without our clothes on."

"But still…"

"C'mon. Breakfast awaits."

The café was small, and pickup trucks that looked ready for a construction site filled the parking lot. The tables were full of working men talking loudly and laughing.

"This must be a good place," Jill said. "The locals eat here."

A cop sitting at a corner table with a cup of coffee nodded to me, and I steered Jill to his table. "You two on duty?" He stood and held the chair for Jill. Then we all sat.

Jill smiled. "A real gentleman. Thank you."

"We're catching breakfast before we go to the park. I'm Doug Fletcher, and this is my partner, Jill."

"D'Wayne Jackson." D'Wayne's leather was spit-polished, and his complexion was as dark as his black leather belt.

Jill looked around. "This must be a good place to eat."

D'Wayne passed menus to us. "It's the only place open for the early-to-work crowd."

"You look like you're just coming on your shift."

D'Wayne smiled. "Why, because I look bright-eyed and bushy-tailed?"

Jill shook her head. "Your uniform looks like it just came off the ironing board."

"Yeah, my pants hold a crease for about thirty seconds in this humidity."

"What do you suggest?" Jill asked, looking through the menu.

"Everything is good. I'm partial to huevos rancheros with hot sauce."

"We're stationed in Texas, but we've still got Midwestern taste buds."

Laughing, D'Wayne waved to a waitress and signaled for coffee. "I assume you take it black like most law enforcement folks."

"Yeah," I replied. "When I worked undercover, I'd go through a dozen cups a night, and I didn't need the calories in cream and sugar."

"Amen," D'Wayne said, nodding.

The waitress brought two mugs and a coffee pot. "Y'all having the same as D'Wayne?" she asked as she poured.

Jill set the menu aside. "Denver omelet with whole-wheat toast, and my partner's having the same."

The waitress sped away, winding through the tables and topping off coffees.

"I'm having an omelet?"

"With veggies inside and whole-wheat toast."

D'Wayne laughed. "You two must've worked together a long time. You sound like a married couple."

Jill smiled. "We are married."

"No shit?"

I nodded. "Although, I'm not sure it's going to last."

Jill's head spun. "Why would you say that?"

"I thought you were going to kill me this morning."

Jill turned to D'Wayne. "Would you expect your wife to look out a window without clothes on?"

D'Wayne put up his hands. "I don't think I want to get between you two on this."

"Just answer the question. Would your wife peek out a bedroom window in the nude?"

"I don't see that happening."

Jill turned to me. "See. It's unreasonable to expect me to check outside without getting dressed."

D'Wayne looked at me. "There's got to be more to the story."

"I heard something outside our cabin, and we grabbed our weapons. I was checking one window for someone sneaking around, and *my partner* decided she wanted to get dressed because she doesn't want to get shot in the nude."

D'Wayne's face lit up, and he started to laugh. "That's what my wife would do, exactly."

"But your wife isn't a cop," I protested.

"Doug, it wouldn't matter if the end of the world was at hand. My wife will get dressed to meet St. Peter."

We talked and laughed through breakfast, explaining our history and why we were in Florida. D'Wayne shared some war stories and offered to help if we needed assistance or backup.

We shook hands after eating, and D'Wayne motioned for us to lean close. "Be careful. You're not from here, and it's a different place than you're used to. People will smile and pretend to be nice, but a lot of them don't like cops or outsiders, and you're both."

# Chapter 6

Speaking on his cell phone, Hawk nodded as we pulled into the preserve headquarters parking lot. He ended the call as we got out of our rental car. "You two had D'Wayne Jackson in stitches with the story about Jill having to get dressed before checking for an intruder outside your cabin."

Jill looked surprised. "Do you know D'Wayne well?"

Sliding the cell phone into his pocket, Hawk nodded. "D'Wayne's Black and I'm Indian, and we're both rare minorities in law enforcement."

I nodded. "You'd trust D'Wayne to back you up."

"I'd trust D'Wayne to leave his breakfast behind to back me up."

Jill appeared shocked. "You think some other cops would finish their meal before they'd respond to your call for assistance?"

"I didn't say that. I *know* D'Wayne would respond without delay, as I would for him."

"You can depend on Doug and me."

Hawk didn't look convinced.

I stared into his eyes. "Hawk, I worked side-by-side with a Navajo Nation PD officer on two investigations. He's my best friend, and I'd lay down my life for him. I'd do the same for you or any other law enforcement professional."

Changing the topic, Hawk opened his pickup door and took out a map. He spread it on the hood and flattened it. "We're here, on the loop past the preserve headquarters." He slid his finger to the right. "The drilling is going on here. Let's see if the protesters are there today."

Hawk was ready to refold the map, but Jill stopped him. "What else is around here?"

"Everything north of here is part of the preserve, until you cross I-95. Beyond the preserve are private ranches and orchards. They're spread out and interspersed with some smaller farming operations. Northeast of here, on the north side of the Tamiami Trail and straddling I-95, is the Miccosukee reservation. If you follow the Tamiami Trail farther east, there are Florida wildlife management areas, and then you hit Sweetwater and the start of the Miami suburbs."

Jill ran her finger over the preserve. "There aren't many roads."

"The Everglades and Big Cypress Preserve have some of the most inaccessible areas in the lower forty-eight states. Most of the preserve is inaccessible except by 4-wheelers in winter and airboats in summer. Even if you can get through, everything looks the same, and it's easy to get lost."

"Does that happen often?" I asked.

Hawk folded the map. "Not that we know of."

Jill cocked her head. "That's not the same as no."

The corner of Hawk's mouth twitched. "No, it's not."

* * *

The drive to the drill site was boring. The Tamiami Trail appeared like it had been scooped out of the swamp, creating a hump with watery ditches on both sides. Beyond the trenches, cypress trees surrounded the hillocks, their "knees," which were roots that split from the main tree trunk, rose above the waterline and extended into the water. Openings in the cypress forest gave us glimpses of waterways like we'd seen in the Everglades National Park.

Watching my gaze, Hawk sensed my question. "Yes, those are waterways you can kayak or canoe for miles."

From the back, Jill added, "And would never be seen again."

"A Subaru with kayak racks had parked along here a couple years ago. When it became clear the owners probably weren't on an overnight camping trip, I traced the Indiana license plates and spoke with the male owner's parents. They confirmed that their son and daughter-in-law were on a Florida vacation and had planned to kayak the Keys and Everglades."

"Did you find them?" Jill asked.

Hawk shook his head. "We launched an airboat and searched the main waterways on both sides of the road, but the search party never found a trace of them. I assume they got into some side waterways, got turned around, and couldn't find their way back."

"There wasn't any sign of foul play?" I asked.

"The car had been locked up, and their gear was gone. There wasn't blood or any sign of a crime committed."

"They didn't call in for help?" Jill asked.

Glancing in the rearview mirror, Hawk said, "Some cell carriers don't have coverage outside the Miami area."

Jill took out her phone. "I've got one bar of service here."

"You've got one of the carriers who cover this area."

The protest group was small; a woman and three men. They sat on the edge of the

85

road until they saw us approaching and then stood and picked up their placards. Hawk stopped a few yards short of the driveway they were picketing. I heard and felt the deep rumble of the drilling operation, although the drilling rig was out of sight.

Leading the way, Hawk put on his uniform cap and nodded to the protesters like they were acquaintances. "Hey, guys. How's it going?"

The shortest male protester, dressed in tattered shorts and a frayed t-shirt, shook his head. "There's not much traffic today, and only one car honked as they passed."

The woman's outfit was a bit less distressed. Her limbs were deeply tanned, and she wore a wide-brimmed hat. Oversized sunglasses hid her eyes. She wrinkled her nose. "I wish people were more concerned about this. The oil company is raping the land, and the Park Service is letting them do it."

Hawk nodded. "Robyn, you know the courts have the final say. All we rangers can do is follow the law."

Although her eyes were hidden, the woman turned her head, apparently staring at Jill. "Who are *you* guys?"

"We're investigating the disappearance of the missing surveyors. Do you guys know anything about what happened to them?"

All four shook their heads, but Robyn spoke, "We're non-violent, although I can't say I'm disappointed that more of the rapists are out of the picture."

"Did you see anything suspicious the day they disappeared?" I asked.

They all shook their heads, but the female protester answered, "We're here every day, so we don't even know where they were surveying."

"You were here the day they disappeared?" I asked.

"Some of us were here, and the rest were back at the house."

Jill looked around. "You don't have a car. Do you walk here from your house?"

The tallest man was freckled and wore a long-sleeve shirt and long white pants, obviously protecting his light complexion from the Florida sun. "There's no place to park off the road, so we take turns shuttling each other here."

"Was there a different group here the day the surveyors disappeared?" I asked.

The woman looked at the others, nodded at the redhead, and then answered, "Sean and I were here with K.C. and Pat."

Jill was about to say something when I cut her off. "Did you see the surveyors' truck that day?"

Robyn shook her head. "They were working west of here."

Hawk wore a slight smile, understanding where my line of questions headed. Jill looked annoyed, crossing her arms but biting her tongue.

"How far is that from here?"

The woman looked at the others. "I suppose it's fifteen miles from here."

"Is that the direction of your house?"

Sean shook his head, but Robyn cocked hers. "Ranger Washington knows where we stay."

"We just got here, and he hasn't mentioned where you're staying."

The short man started to say something, but the woman cut him off. "Shut up, Kirk." She turned, facing me, and took a step forward. "I told you, we're nonviolent. What are you getting at?"

I raised my hands. "I'm just trying to get to know you. I'm Doug Fletcher, and this is my partner, Jill."

Robyn stretched out her arm with her hand facing the men, signaling for them to stay silent. "I'm not your friend, and I don't appreciate getting interrogated."

Jill stepped forward at the perfect moment. "We're trying to uncover what happened to the surveyors. Your group is out here every day, so you may be the only ones who've seen the people involved in their disappearance."

Sean ignored Robyn's signal not to speak. "We see a few dozen tourists a day and a mix of local folks, mostly driving beat-up pickups. I don't recall anything unusual the day the surveyors disappeared. Are you sure they didn't just drive away, and something happened to them in Sweetwater or Everglades City?"

"You didn't see their truck pass here," I said. "So, they wouldn't be anywhere east of here. And having said you didn't see them pass tells me you've seen their truck in the past, so you know what it looks like."

Robyn dropped her arm, then turned her head toward Sean, a signal for him to shut up. She took off her sunglasses, exposing a swollen black eye. She glared at me. "We don't appreciate your bullshit cop interrogation."

Jill stepped forward, looking concerned. "Robyn, what happened to your eye?"

Robyn fumbled with her glasses and put them back on, apparently feeling she'd exposed something she shouldn't have. "I walked into a door in the dark."

A look passed between the guys, but none spoke.

"Can I look at it again?" Jill asked.

Robyn shook her head as I glanced at her arms and legs, noticing bruising on her upper arms and shins. "Did the door grab you by the arms and kick you?"

Sean blew out a breath. "One of the local yokels recognized her in the grocery store."

89

"And?" Jill asked, stepping up to the woman and touching the bruises on her left arm.

"And he'd had a little too much to drink," Sean said. "He…"

Robyn pulled off her sunglasses and turned her swollen eye toward Jill. "He grabbed me by the arm and said I might enjoy a ride in his pickup. I said I wasn't going anywhere and shoved him. He punched me and tried to drag me out of the store."

Sean shook his head. "I heard the commotion and rushed to the front of the store. By then, a cashier and the produce guy had stepped in and shoved the yokel out the door."

"What did the cops say?" Jill asked.

Robyn sniffled and put her sunglasses back on. "No one called the cops. The store clerk said there was no point."

Jill looked at Hawk, who shrugged. "Like I said, the locals don't like outsiders."

We returned to the truck, and Hawk started the engine, causing a blast of hot air. Jill slammed the back door and looked at Hawk in the rearview mirror. "What would've happened if the yokel had got Robyn into his truck?"

"Nothing good."

Putting her hand on my shoulder, Jill asked, "Why didn't you want me to interrupt your questions?"

"None of us said which day the surveyors disappeared, but they knew. I wanted to see if they'd say how they knew, or maybe reveal more than that."

The protesters had set their signs down and gathered in a huddle, obviously discussing something about our interaction. Hawk watched them. "I wish I could read lips. They're having a heated discussion, and I wonder what they're talking about."

Jill leaned her arms on the seatback. "Are they safe out here? You said the locals carry guns and don't like outsiders."

"They're gone from here before sunset, and there's enough of them staying in the old house that no one's going to bother them."

Jill drew a breath. "Unlike the surveyors, who were alone and out of sight."

Hawk looked at her. "Yeah, like that." Checking his mirrors, he pulled onto the road. "Would you like to see what the preserve is really like off the road?"

Jill slid back and buckled her seat belt. "Yes!"

"There's a loop road that turns south in a couple miles. I usually drive it once a day to make sure some hapless tourist didn't get stuck in a muddy spot."

The turn for the loop road was well marked. "What's down this road?"

"Scenic Everglades beauty," Hawk replied.

"Is there a town here?" Jill asked as we turned onto a muddy road that wasn't wide enough for two cars to meet.

"No towns. No gas stations. Pretty much nothing but birds, gators, and an occasional tourist, who mistakenly thought the road would improve after the first muddy stretch."

Hawk drove slowly, doing a slalom around puddles and holes where rental cars had scraped bottom. The vegetation was dense and felt jungle-like. Then, the scenery changed to a cedar swamp with open water. A black alligator lay on a fallen log, unbothered by our passing. Spooked by our approach, a flock of white birds flew through the cypress canopy. A black-crowned night heron stood in shallow water watching us warily. Farther down the road, an egret grabbed a small silver fish out of the water and flew away.

"This is beautiful, Hawk," Jill said from the back seat.

Hawk stopped the truck and shifted into park. "Jill, please open the cooler and pass around the sandwiches."

Jill shuffled around in the back and pulled a cooler from behind the driver's seat. "We're having a picnic?"

"I threw together a few sandwiches and some bottled water in case we got delayed somewhere remote, like this."

Jill passed sandwiches, bottles of water, and bags of potato chips to Hawk and me. "What are we having?" she asked.

"I'm in a rut," Hawk replied, pulling his sandwich out of a plastic bag. "I have a fried Spam sandwich almost every day." He took a bite and ripped open the potato chip bag.

"Thanks," I said, holding up my sandwich. "I haven't had a Spam sandwich since I was a kid."

I glanced at Jill, who had the most pained smile I'd ever seen on her face. She took a tiny bite, chewed, and continued to smile. "I had Spam and eggs for breakfast when I was in Hawaii a decade ago and was amazed that Hawaii eats more Spam than any other state. I guess it's a carryover from World War II when meat was shipped from the mainland, and Spam became a treat."

Hawk wolfed down his sandwich before Jill finished chewing her second bite. "Spam sandwiches don't need refrigeration like a lot of other things, and sometimes I keep them in the cooler for two days without worry."

I looked at Jill, who'd stopped chewing. "These are two days old?"

"Naw, I made these this morning and threw them in the cooler with frozen water bottles. These are fresh."

Jill politely ate her sandwich but gave me a look that said we'd find other lunch options in the future.

Finishing off the last potato chip crumbs and ready to start driving again, Hawk said, "A lot of people think we need to pull the plug and drain the water so the land will be useful."

I looked at an alligator lying on the edge of the road, and it didn't even move as we passed within a foot of him. "He seems tame."

Laughing, Hawk slowed so Jill could slide across the seat to see the large reptile. "A lot of tourists think they can get out of the cars to take pictures."

"Yeah," Jill said from the back seat. "Last week, a woman tried to put her kid on a gator for a picture down in the Everglades National Park."

"I assume that didn't go well."

"She suffered a broken leg, and the kid has some scrapes." Jill paused. "The first park I worked in had free-ranging animals, and some idiot always ignored the signs to get a closeup with his wife and kids standing near a buffalo."

"I read about someone getting gored by a buffalo in the Black Hills last year."

"A woman got too close to a buffalo calf, and a bull hooked her belt, throwing her around like a rag doll until the belt broke."

A silver rental car, its sides mud-splattered, came bouncing toward us. The driver lowered his window as we met. "Are we getting close to the end?" asked the young male driver.

"You're closer to the end than the beginning," Hawk replied.

"Does the road get any better?"

"It doesn't get worse if that's any consolation."

The guy nodded, rolled up his window, and splashed away behind us.

We drove on, Hawk skirting mud holes in the road, and me considering the vast expanse beyond us. We passed an open span of water with deadfall trees hanging over it. Four black anhingas, their wings spread wide, perched on a deadfall.

Stopping the truck, Hawk asked, "You guys know about the anhingas, right?"

"They're the black birds perched back there," I replied.

"They don't have oil glands like other aquatic birds, so their feathers get soaked with water. They perch with their wings spread to dry out after diving for fish."

Amazed that Jill would ride silently for half an hour, I turned to see if she was napping in the back seat.

"What?"

"I thought you'd fallen asleep."

"I was thinking about the protester who had gotten attacked in the grocery store."

"And what do you think about that?"

"It says a lot about the contempt locals have for the protesters. There's a local guy whose inhibitions become lowered with alcohol, and he's brazen enough to drag her out of the store. Then, there's the store manager, who's unwilling to call the cops on a local idiot that assaulted a protester."

Hawk glanced in the mirror. "Don't paint all the local people with the same brush. There are nice, polite, hard-working people here, and I'm sure there are people back in the Black Hills who act stupid when they drink, too."

I heard Jill sigh. "You're right, there are drunken idiots everywhere, and I shouldn't characterize everyone here as a redneck. It's just hard for me to get my head around the open hostility shown toward the protesters. They're quietly protesting what they see as the oil companies despoiling this undisturbed preserve. They're not hurting anyone or damaging anything."

Slowing to ease around a particularly muddy spot, Hawk was in quiet contemplation. "It's not just that they're protesters. They're privileged outsiders. They've been here for months without working or any visible means of support.

They drive foreign cars, and there's a dozen of them, men and women, living together in a commune. I hear rumors that they're having orgies, using drugs, and living like a bunch of hippies. None of those things sit well with the people hanging out in the bars."

"Aah," Jill said from the back seat. "They're left-wing liberals in a place that's staunchly Republican."

I chuckled. "It reminds me of Europeans being concerned about the gypsies. Are the local folks afraid the protesters are going to kidnap their children and convert them into communists?"

"Doug," Hawk said without smiling, "you might've found the perfect analogy."

We finished the loop road without encountering any stranded rental cars, although I was surprised the rental car we'd seen hadn't gotten stuck in one of the muddy areas. "Most of the parks post signs on roads like this saying that they're minimal maintenance, so people know they're going to have a rough ride."

Hawk chuckled. "The maps given out by the car rental companies show this road in red. The inset warns drivers that any car damage incurred while driving on red roads is not covered by the optional insurance, and your credit card will receive the charge."

"When I was the Flagstaff superintendent, a guy had rented a Jeep and was driving the arroyos and rolled it. It cost a thousand bucks to get a tow truck out to haul it back to the rental place. I heard his credit card got charged for the value of the Jeep and the lost rental days until they replaced it."

"Whew," Hawk said. "I suppose his car insurance reimbursed him."

"He was from New York, so he didn't own a car, so didn't have insurance. I think he was stuck with the $30,000 charged to his VISA card."

"Ouch," Hawk said as he pulled into the visitor center parking lot. He parked next to our rental car, and we climbed out. "What would you like to do tomorrow?"

I looked at Jill, who shrugged. "I don't suppose you have a helicopter that could look for the surveyors' truck."

"We don't have a helicopter, nor do we have money to rent one."

"Where is the surveyors' office? I'd like to ask them if they've received any threats."

"I think they worked out of an office in Everglades City. I'll check it out tonight and have an address by morning." Hawk paused. "I can pick you up at the campground office in the morning, rather than having you drive here, then double back."

We agreed to that plan, then stood next to the rental car, waiting for the air conditioning to cool it off. Jill leaned her arms on the roof, then jumped back when she felt the searing heat. "It's Thursday and our return flight is Saturday. Do we rebook now, or do you think we'll either solve this or give up tomorrow?"

"I think we're going to get hit with a rebooking fee if we change our flights now or if we wait until an hour before the flight. Let's just leave the itinerary as is and hope for the best."

Considering that thought, Jill wrinkled her nose. "We really have no idea how long this is going to take."

"Not really," I said, getting into the still-hot seat.

"When do we throw in the towel?"

"We're only two days into the investigation, and you're ready to throw in the towel?"

Jill remained silent until we were on the highway. "I felt more confident about finding the Iowans, who aliens had abducted than I am about locating this survey crew."

"Why?"

"This place is so desolate and unforgiving. I can understand how people disappear and never get found here. There are hundreds of thousands of acres of swamps, filled with critters, who'll eat anything they can kill, and others that will eat anything that's already dead." Jill paused. "Then, there are the human predators."

Jill continued mulling those thoughts when I pulled into Joanie's parking lot. I unbuckled and opened my car door.

"We're eating here again?"

"The next restaurant is ten miles away, and I'm perfectly happy eating here. The food is tasty and wholesome, and the prices are reasonable."

"It's okay, but I don't need a slice of key lime pie. I haven't burned off the last one yet." We got in line and checked the chalkboard for the daily special. "What is she-crab soup?"

The man ahead of us turned and said, "It's made from crab meat and crab roe. There's nothing better on this earth than Joanie's she-crab soup."

After the man turned away, Jill mouthed, "Crab roe soup?"

Joanie spotted us in line and winked at me. The line slowly diminished as diners finished their meals, and the waitress cleared tables. When we got to the front of the line, Joanie leaned across the counter to Jill. "The she-crab soup is one of our specialties. It's got about a cup of cream in each bowlful. If you'd like something lighter, I've got some wonderful grouper. The cook can whip up a grilled grouper sandwich if you'd prefer that."

Joanie spotted a couple leaving a booth in the back corner and led us through the chattering crowd. Two tourists noticed my badge and gun, nodding as we passed. A table of young men glared as we passed, one of them whispering to his buddies.

A waitress, old enough to be my mother, swept up to the table and cleared the dishes left by the previous diners. "I don't know why Joanie set you at a dirty table, but if you give me just a second, I'll get these plates cleared and bring you something to drink."

"Unsweet tea and a grilled grouper sandwich," Jill said.

The gray-haired waitress looked at me. "I'll bet you want a long neck."

"That, and a bowl of she-crab soup. Thanks."

The waitress wiped our table and sped away with the dirty dishes, threading her way through the crowded room.

Jill leaned across. "That was kind of Joanie to get us this booth in the back."

"Yeah, I wouldn't want to be sitting back-to-back with the table of guys we passed on the way in."

Jill nodded. "The ones that keep glancing at us and whispering among themselves?"

"Yeah, them."

A boy, no more than ten or eleven, came out of the men's bathroom, looking embarrassed. Sliding into the booth behind us, he started whispering to his mother. It all happened behind Jill's back. I watched the bathroom door to see if someone came out looking guilty, but no one else appeared.

Jill straightened up, then leaned back a bit, listening to the whispered conversation behind her. She stifled a laugh and leaned forward. "I think you need to check out the men's restroom."

"Why?"

She shook her head. "Just go."

I slid out of the booth and walked past a table where three kids and their parents were scanning the eclectic mixture of junk hanging from the walls and playing "I spy with my little eye." The mom looked around the room, gave a hint about something she could see, and the kids fired off the names of items that matched the clue—all having fun while they waited for their meals.

Opening the restroom door, I immediately knew why the boy had whispered to his mother. The walls were covered with pictures of buxom, topless biker chicks. I chuckled, thinking about the overwhelmed youngster who probably hadn't ever seen a bare-breasted woman.

Jill greeted me with a smug grin when I returned. "Well?"

"Dozens of topless women, none less than a DD." I paused while she laughed.

"Your turn. I wonder what pictures are in the women's bathroom."

Jill shook her head. "They don't put bawdy pictures in women's bathrooms."

"Why not?"

"Women don't appreciate seeing naked men."

"I think the Chippendales performances always sell out." When Jill didn't respond, I said, "Just go in the bathroom and tell me what's on the walls."

Jill slid out of the booth. "You're going to be disappointed." She was back in five minutes, shaking her head. "Hunky cowboys, all very tasteful," she whispered as she slid into the booth.

"I don't believe you."

Our dinner arrived before she responded. "Your soup smells wonderful," Jill said as she unfolded her napkin and spread it on her lap.

Jill made appreciative noises as she ate the grouper sandwich. "Hawk has me a little spooked. Let's go back to the gas station and fill up. There's a convenience store there, and we can buy some things for breakfast and put them in the little refrigerator at the cottage."

"Do you have a hidden agenda?"

"Like what?"

"Buying something for lunch, so you don't have to eat another Spam sandwich."

Jill grimaced. "I'd forgotten how salty Spam tastes. I mean, it was nice of him to pack lunches for us, and Spam is probably a good option when you don't have refrigeration, but it wouldn't be my first choice for lunch."

"Or breakfast, supper, or snacking."

Jill ate her last piece of grouper. "Yeah, pretty much. Why are we going to the survey company?"

"It's a loose end. They may know more about what the surveyors were doing."

"Hawk said they've been surveying oil leases."

"I'd like to know exactly where those surveys have been done and if they've had any other work besides the drilling leases."

\* \* \*

I gassed up while Jill checked out the convenience store's breakfast options. She returned with two plastic shopping bags.

I buckled my seat belt and started the engine. "Looks like you found a lot of breakfast supplies."

"I got a few things for each of us."

"That means I don't have to eat horse feed and yogurt like you do?"

"It's granola, and it's not just oats."

"Excuse me? It's horse feed and other added ingredients."

"You're hopeless. I got you two microwavable breakfast sandwiches, and they look like they're oozing grease and full of nitrates and preservatives."

"Perfect!"

"I also got orange juice and more coffee for the miniature coffee maker. I think it only cost us slightly more than a week of restaurant breakfasts."

"They call it a convenience store because you pay for the convenience."

Jill got silent, and I glanced at her. "What's wrong?"

"I'm thinking about the surveyors. What do you think happened to them?"

"I don't think they're alive if that's what you're asking."

"I suppose not, but why were they killed, and where are their bodies?" Jill paused. "What about their truck and gear?"

"What about it?"

"Hawk pointed out that it's easy enough to dispose of bodies here just by dumping them in the swamp. But where's their truck? Alligators and buzzards don't eat pickups."

"I suspect when we find either the bodies or the truck, we'll know what happened to the other."

"You said, 'when we find,' not if we find. You're confident we're going to locate something?"

"Surveyors carry a lot of very expensive laser equipment and probably computers to record what they're doing. I think even a drug addict would understand the intrinsic value of the equipment and try to sell it."

"Do you think this was a drug crime?"

"Not really. I was using a drug addict as the lowest possible level of criminal who'd realize the value of the surveyors' equipment."

"What if it was a drug addict?"

"I doubt an addict would shoot the victims. I think there's something else in play here."

"I can't see the protesters killing the surveyors. Like they said, they're into non-violent picketing."

I drew a breath. "It's too early to rule anyone out, but I think you're probably right. There's something more."

"Not the oil companies. The surveyors were marking out the leases for them."

"I want to know what the surveyors were doing in the days and weeks before they disappeared. I think the answer is in their activities."

The moon, partially obscured by clouds, offered just enough light to guide us down the pathway. I stopped short of the cabin, causing Jill to bump into me.

"Geez, you don't have brake lights. Give me some warning before you make an emergency stop."

I gently set down the convenience store bags. I put my finger to my lips, realizing it was a useless gesture because I could barely see Jill's face. "There's a light on in the cabin," I whispered.

"We probably left it on when we left this morning."

I drew my gun. "I made sure the lights were all off. Get out your cell phone and wait here. I'll check it out."

I heard the sound of Jill's Glock pistol drawn from her holster. "Like hell I'm waiting here in the dark wondering what's going on." She pushed my shoulder.

I stopped next to one of the windows and peeked inside, assuming whoever was there wouldn't be able to see outside. The room seemed empty.

Jill pushed next to me. "Anything?"

"Shh."

I felt a jab in my ribs, then a push on my shoulder. I eased up the steps, staying along the right edge. Jill monitored the window, watching inside. The click of the door lock sounded like a gunshot in the silence. Knowing whatever I'd done to be quiet was now lost, I threw the door open, swinging my pistol from side to side.

There was a small table near the coffee maker with a stack of fresh towels, shampoo, and two water bottles. Propped against the towel pile was a handwritten note from our housekeeper encouraging us to call the front desk if we needed anything.

Hearing Jill's footsteps on the porch, I realized how useless my attempt at stealth had been. The door creaked open. "What did you find?"

"Fresh towels and bottled water."

Jill's tension broke, and she laughed. "Towels?"

I gestured toward the pile of linens and holstered my gun while Jill turned on more lights. Jill was about to say something when I heard a noise outside. The noise was familiar but somehow seemed out of context.

Jill dashed for the door. "The groceries!"

Grabbing a flashlight from the bedside table, I followed Jill out the door. A waddling animal with a banded tail flashed past as Jill reached for the bags we'd set on the ground.

Jill gathered the bags and some scattered wrappers from the ground as I lit the area with the flashlight. Setting the bags on the table next to the stack of towels, Jill removed the contents. "Looks like raccoons prefer sausage biscuits to granola and yogurt."

"Shit."

"There is some good news. The little varmint left the beer and popcorn I bought for watching television tonight."

# Chapter 7

Hawk was waiting for us in the campground parking lot. Jill claimed the front seat after a day of riding in the back. "How are you this morning, Hawk?"

"I'm good," he said and then paused and looked at me in the rearview mirror. "You look unhappy, Doug."

Jill jumped in before I responded. "He's cranky because he had to eat granola and yogurt for breakfast."

Hawk glanced at her as he pulled onto the Tamiami Trail, driving west toward Everglades City. "That sounds healthy."

"Doug's mad because raccoons ate his sausage biscuits last night, so he had to eat healthy food with me this morning."

"*Someone* left the bags with the biscuits on the ground, and the raccoons had a smorgasbord. Strangely, they didn't bother with the yogurt Jill bought for herself."

Hawk laughed. "I've heard animals won't eat yogurt. It smells spoiled."

"It's sour milk! Wild animals are smart enough to know that."

Jill twisted in her seat. "Just let it go, okay?"

Like most NPS vehicles, the radio in the pickup was tuned to a frequency reserved for transmissions from headquarters or between rangers. It had been quiet for nearly two days until chimes sounded. Hawk reached for the controls and changed the frequency.

"What's up?" Jill asked.

"Those were the emergency tones from the Florida Highway Patrol. Listen."

The dispatcher announced a pursuit in progress on Highway 29, going north from Everglades City. Then she requested any available units to assist.

Hawk pressed the accelerator and turned on the flashers. "They'll likely go up the coast, toward Naples. We might get to Carnestown before they pass."

"Where's Carnestown?" Jill asked.

"It's the gas station and C-store at the crossroads of 29 and Tamiami Trail."

"Ah, where we bought groceries last night."

Hawk didn't respond, concentrating on his driving as he passed rental cars. He picked up the mic and reported that we'd just passed the airboat concession a few miles west of the preserve entrance. He slowed as the driver ahead of us was oblivious to the red and blue flashers behind him, and several cars were coming toward us.

"There's not really a shoulder for anyone to turn onto," Jill observed.

Hawk finally passed the slow car and accelerated hard. "All the road material had gotten trucked in, and the builders were more focused on completing the highway than adding frills, like a shoulder."

We listened as more highway patrol units called in, mostly coming south from the Naples area. The dispatcher provided an update. "The suspect vehicle is a white van, and the perpetrators driving it fired at the Coast Guard boat pursuing them before transferring to the van."

"Does this happen often?" Jill asked.

"The drug-running or the pursuit?"

"Both, I guess."

"There are a thousand islands between Florida City and Naples. Mexican and South American drug smugglers bring their ocean-going ships close to the islands and drop cargo onto smaller boats able to evade the Coast Guard cutters in island backwaters. That happens a couple times a month. The Coasties cut some smugglers off before they get to shore, but we assume many slip through at night unnoticed. I'm guessing a boat had engine trouble, so got caught crossing to the shore during daylight."

"And the chase?"

"This is the first in quite a while. I don't usually get involved because most go straight up Highway 29, and they're usually past Tamiami Trail before I can get there."

The pursuing highway patrolman announced the mile marker he was passing. "How close is that to Carnestown?" I asked.

Hawk glanced at me in the mirror. "We're closer than he is."

Hawk announced our location and said we would block the road at Carnestown. The dispatcher announced Hawk's plan. The trooper in pursuit responded. "Park Service. Deploy stop sticks rather than setting up a roadblock."

Hawk chuckled and picked up the mic. "Stop sticks are not emergency equipment we carry, Hal."

"Hal's the trooper we met at Joanie's the day we met you," Jill said.

Hawk nodded as the trooper replied, "Block him from proceeding north on 29. If we can force him onto Tamiami Trail, his big ole' van is probably gonna run outta gas before he gets to the other end."

Hawk acknowledged the request, then glanced at Jill. "Get away from the vehicle as soon as I stop. The driver might be on whatever he's hauling, and there's no guarantee Hal's plan is going to work."

I unbuckled my seat belt as the crossroads stoplights came into sight. "Most plans sound good when you talk them through, but bad guys don't always follow the script."

Hawk slowed as we approached the stoplights. In the distance, I saw the white van with two sets of flashing lights following it. "Jump out here and run to the gas station." He pulled into the intersection, blocking the northbound highway, leaving a turn onto Tamiami Trail as the van's obvious option.

The van closed on us fast, leaving no time to get out of the pickup and get clear of a potential crash. We'd be on the grassy shoulders, a likely route for the van if he were committed to continuing north.

"No time to bail," I said as I re-buckled my seat belt. "Brace for a crash."

The van slowed as it approached, allowing me to see the interaction between driver and passenger. The passenger gestured toward the back, and the driver pointed to his right, toward the Tamiami Trail.

I braced my feet against the back of the seat and leaned away from the potential impact on the driver's side of the pickup. Jill leaned forward and wrapped her arms around her knees. Hawk leaned toward Jill.

The van crossed the centerline as if planning to go around the front of the pickup. The driver cranked the steering wheel right, and the van's tires screeched as the vehicle leaned, then teetered on two wheels as the momentum wanted to carry the weight forward while the tires grabbed the road.

"Oh shit," Hawk said. "He's going to flip and slide into us."

The tires won the battle of physics as the van's rear slid and turned it broadside with the rear tires smoking. The van continued sliding, then turned east. I saw the two pursuing troopers slow and weave as they waited for the impending crash.

The van teetered leaning toward us and then swung right. It missed the pickup's rear bumper by less than a foot before turning and rumbling across the grassy shoulder of the Tamiami Trail for twenty yards before gaining control and steering onto the blacktop road. It narrowly missed an oncoming pickup. The van sped to the east with the two troopers screeching around the corner behind it.

Hawk jammed the transmission into reverse, and after a quick three-point-turn, our tires spun on the grass. The pickup lurched ahead when the tires bit the blacktop. Hawk made a tight loop around the intersection and accelerated forward on the Tamiami Trail as the pursuit sped away from us, going east.

Jill was up, orienting herself to what had happened while her head was down, bracing for the crash. "They turned?"

Hawk wrestled with the wheel as he steered around the oncoming pickup, who had pulled far onto the edge of the road as the van and troopers cars sped past. Hawk waved at the driver, then accelerated.

Gripping her seat belt shoulder strap with her left hand, Jill reached up for the overhead "oh shit" handle with her right hand. "Can we catch them?"

Our engine raced and the transmission strained as it shifted through the gears. "We've got a lot more horsepower than the van and should catch up in a couple miles."

Jill had never been in a high-speed chase before, and her tension grew palpable. "Why don't the troopers force him off the road?"

"There's not enough real estate alongside the road to do a PIT maneuver. The van and trooper's car could both end up in the channel."

"So, what are they going to do?"

"They'll follow the van until it runs out of gas or until a trooper from Sweetwater gets ahead of them and places stop sticks."

Jill appeared taut and focused, breathing shallow, and her knuckles turned white. Nearing the second of the trooper's cars, Hawk backed off the gas and maintained a position far enough behind so he could stop without hitting the trooper in front of us.

"Do you think these guys might have something to do with our missing surveyors? You've always said the biggest murder motives are love, money, and drugs."

Glancing at me in the rearview mirror, Hawk thought, then answered, "I doubt it. These guys are smuggling drugs, and I don't know why they'd bother with a couple of surveyors."

"Maybe the surveyors were part of their smuggling operation."

The van and pursuit vehicles resembled a high-speed parade as they swerved around tourists' cars. "I guess we can keep that in the back of our minds, but my gut says this is unrelated to the surveyors."

The dispatcher announced that the Coast Guard Opa Locka station had a helicopter in the air and should be approaching our position in ten minutes.

"Where's Opa Locka?" I asked from the back seat.

"It's an executive airport south of Miami. It used to be a military base, but they turned it over to Dade County and the Coast Guard."

Tapping the brakes, Hawk started to slow. "The idiot is passing a car, and there's a minivan coming in the other lane."

I leaned forward to see ahead, but Hawk's shoulders blocked my view. A second later, I was thrown against the seat belt when Hawk jammed the brakes. The trooper in front moved right, and his tires went off the road in danger of rolling into the canal. As Hawk followed him, I got a brief glimpse of the white van cutting off the tourist ahead of us and clipping the front bumper of an oncoming minivan.

The minivan violently spun into the side of the white van. As often happened when viewing something violent and unexpected, the collision played out in slow motion. The minivan's momentum turned into a spectacular roll that flipped it onto its side, sliding down the road in a shower of sparks.

My focus remained on the innocent minivan until I heard Jill gasp. She watched the rest of the collision playing out ahead of us. The lead trooper rammed the back of the car that had been cut off by the white van. Past the trooper, I saw the top of the van veer toward the canal. The back of it hopped up just before it disappeared down the embankment.

I unbuckled the seat belt before the pickup stopped. "Call for an ambulance, Hawk." My request was unnecessary because Hawk lifted the mic as I spoke. I heard one of the troopers reporting the crash and requesting assistance.

I jumped out of the back and raced to the minivan. The airbags had deployed, and I saw the front seat occupants pushing at the white fabric as I approached. I knelt and saw the man and woman in the front seat dangling from their seat belts. They seemed dazed but relatively unharmed.

I heard cries from the minivan's back seats but couldn't see past the adults. Out of the corner of my eye, I saw Jill flash past. I looked up as she jumped, landed on her waist and hands on the side of the van. In a second, she threw her legs up and kneeled on the sliding door, pushed herself around, released the latch, and opened the door. Children were crying, and Jill slipped inside the van before I stood.

"Doug, get up here!" she yelled.

Unable to hop up as Jill had, I found footsteps and handholds on the minivan's undercarriage. It felt like minutes later when I was on my hands and knees, sweaty and breathing heavily, finally reaching the open side door. Inside, Jill stood on the opposite window, now against the ground. She whispered to a child in a car seat. The child cried as Jill gently released the straps and pulled the young girl into her arms.

"I'm up here," I said.

She nodded, murmured to the child, then passed her up to me. "There's an unconscious boy by my feet."

"Fletcher, pass her down to me," Hawk said, standing next to the van.

I carefully passed the sobbing girl to Hawk, who pulled her into his arms. Then I bent over the open door and looked down at Jill. She had crouched next to a boy strapped into a booster seat, and she whispered to him, only getting moans in response.

"Is there anyone in the far back seat?" I whispered.

Jill shook her head without looking up. "Check on the parents."

The door handle had been ripped off during the roll, so I struggled to release the latch and open the door. Gravity fought me as I pushed the bashed door against its hinges. The driver, a young man, twisted in his seat to communicate with Jill in the back. I touched his arm, and he turned. His nose bled, and he had cuts where his glasses had been thrown against his face by the airbags.

"Can you release your seat belt without falling against your wife?"

He looked at me like he didn't understand what I said. "My seat belt?"

"Is your wife okay?" I asked, trying a different question.

Looking down, he reached out his right hand, and I saw a woman's hand reach up to grasp it. I heard soft words, then a click as the woman released her seat belt., and she squirmed free and pushed herself up between the seat and dashboard.

Her blonde hair was bloody. Standing, she was nose-to-nose with the man. Before I could say anything, she released her husband's seat belt, and he tumbled headfirst into her seat, almost knocking her down.

I reached out my right hand. "Climb up the seats, and I'll pull you out." She reached out with her right arm, then gasped in pain. I realized it twisted at an unnatural angle. "Use your left hand."

It took a couple of minutes for her to get on top of the van. She was disoriented, clutching her right arm to her side. "Angel. Where's Angel?" she asked as I slid her off the van, into Hawk's grasp."

"I've got Angel, Ma'am. It's okay."

"Where's Ricky?"

Hawk led her to the pickup, and I looked down at Jill. "How are you doing?"

She looked up at me and shook her head. "Unconscious," she whispered. "Heartbeat steady, but his breathing is shallow. I don't think I should move him until the paramedics arrive."

I spun around and looked inside the driver's door. The husband squirmed around, trying to get on his feet. "Climb up the seats," I said, extending my hand to him.

He slowly got upright and climbed out, holding my hand firmly. "Where's Ann?"

"Ann's your wife?"

"Yeah," he said as he sat on the side of the minivan.

"She's with my partner and your daughter in the Park Service pickup." I helped him down, then hung my head over the door where Jill stayed with the boy. "How's he doing?"

"I'm not sure. The seat belt is pressing against his neck, and I think that's part of his breathing problem."

I closed my eyes and prayed it was the cause of the kid's problem. "Do you still want to wait for the paramedics? We're in the middle of nowhere, and it's going to take a while for an ambulance or rescue squad to get here."

As my eyes adjusted to the darkness in the minivan, I saw that Jill supported the boy's head in her hands.

"I don't know. I'd cut him loose if this were a backcountry injury, but all my urban first aid training said to leave injured people in situ. The EMTs can assess him for spinal injuries and stabilize his neck before they extract him."

"I think gas is leaking out of the tank. I think you both need to get out of there, or you'll have a more acute problem."

I heard the click of the seat belt release, and the boy fell into Jill's arms. "I hope we've made the right decision." She lifted the boy's inert body high enough for me to reach. The kid had to weigh more than forty pounds to be in a booster seat instead of a child's car seat and hefting him up while laying on my belly took all my strength.

"Support his neck, Doug."

"I can barely lift him as it is."

Jill must've stepped on something to hoist him because he became lighter. Cradling his head, I slid him onto the side of the minivan. Jill hopped out and mopped her forehead, her shirt clinging from a combination of the heat, humidity, and stress.

"Ease him down and move him into the pickup."

I felt the thumping of the helicopter before I heard it. The orange dot on the eastern horizon quickly grew, and I became aware of shouting. Hawk was nowhere in sight, so we carried the boy to the front seat of the pickup. His parents and sister were in the back talking. The mom attempted to climb over the seat when she saw us carrying her son.

"Ma'am, we want to keep him flat on the seat until the paramedics get here," Jill said gently but firmly.

I left the pickup and ran toward the shouting where Hawk and the two troopers stood off the edge of the road. There was splashing in the canal, and one of the troopers drew his pistol and aimed. Seeing that, I drew my pistol, ran ahead, then took cover behind the front fender of the trooper's car. I scanned the edge of the canal, expecting to see one of the guys from the van holding a gun. Shouts and Spanish curses came from the channel, along with splashing.

"Sonofabitch!" the trooper shouted, then he fired three times.

Hawk, Hal Rude, and the other trooper, drew their guns and repeatedly fired into the canal. I couldn't see anything but rushed to their aid, unprepared for the scene.

The smuggler's van was mainly submerged, with all the front and back doors open. Six or seven people swam or waded toward the roadbed while three big black alligators moved toward the sound of their splashing. One group member was a young woman with a child in her arms. Another, a middle-aged man, water up to his neck, shouted Spanish as he helped others out of the van.

"Fletcher, shoot the gators!" Hawk yelled right before the two troopers opened fire again, emptying their pistols at the black shapes moving toward the splashing people. Waterspouts erupted around the gators. One gator was either hit or annoyed by the gunfire and dove under the surface. I wasn't sure if that was a good or a bad thing.

I scrambled down to the edge of the water, braced my feet as best I could, and started pulling people out of the channel.

My shoulder, injured during an earlier investigation, screamed in pain, but the adrenaline kept me going.

The thump, thump, thump of the helicopter blades was nearly upon us. Almost immediately, the shadow of the orange Coast Guard helicopter darkened the water over the canal, the downwash whipped the surface of the water, and miraculously, the alligators turned and swam away.

Hawk slid down the embankment next to me and helped pull the woman and child up the steep slope. Then a man, arm covered in gang tattoos, reached up for assistance, and I reached past him to pull a teenage girl from behind him.

Hal Rude slid down the embankment with his pistol pointed at the tattooed guy. He rattled off Spanish instructions to the guy, who reluctantly lifted his shirt, exposing a black pistol tucked into his waistband. With encouragement from the trooper, the man carefully removed the pistol with two fingers and threw it onto the embankment.

"What the hell is going on?" I yelled over the sound of the helicopter.

"Coyotes brought in Cubans looking for asylum."

The man helping people exit the rear of the van waved and shouted at us. Between the helicopter noise and my limited

Spanish, I couldn't understand what he was conveying.

A splash to my right startled me; Jill was swimming toward the man like she was the anchor person in the Olympic relays. She placed her hand on the man's shoulder, then pulled something out of the back of the van. With a brightly colored bundle tucked under her arm, she swam toward me.

I waded into the canal and was immediately waist-deep in water. Jill pushed the bundled child toward me. "Start chest compressions!" She turned and swam back to the van as I pulled a young girl into my arms.

I'd barely turned when Hawk took the girl from me. "There are two more!" he yelled.

Jill swam another small person toward shore, followed by the man evacuating people from the back and now dog paddling behind her. Jill pushed a boy into my arms and gasped for breath. "I think this is the last one, but I'm going back to check."

She swam back toward the van before I could tell her not to. Feeling a hand on my shoulder, I passed the limp child to Hal Rude, who took him out of my hands and scrambled up the embankment.

I pulled the dog paddling man to dry ground. "Gracias, Señor. Muchas gracias," the man gasped.

I looked past him at Jill, treading water and catching her breath. Then she dove down next to the van and repeated the process over and over until she finally looked at me and nodded. "I think we got them all." She swam back to shore slowly, obviously tired.

I pulled her toward the dry ground, but instead of climbing the embankment, she pulled me into an embrace. "I don't think those two kids will make it," she whispered into my ear. She clutched me as tightly as she'd ever hugged me.

The moment was so intense that I hardly registered the sounds of the helicopter landing on the roadway. We slogged up the embankment, slipping backward every third or fourth step. At the top, we collapsed.

"Water," Hawk said, holding out a frosty bottle for each of us.

I took it and cracked the seal, drinking deeply. So did Jill. "Thanks," we said at the same time.

Hawk squatted next to me, and we watched the helicopter crew do chest compressions on the boy from the van. In rotation, one crewman squeezed a plastic bag that forced air into the boy's lungs while the partner did fifteen quick chest compressions. The girl who'd gotten out first was coughing and wheezing in a woman's arms.

Hawk looked at Jill and shook his head. "So, your Olympic event was the 50-meter freestyle."

Jill took another swallow of water. "Sometimes it pays to keep in shape."

I looked at the Coast Guard medics treating the boy. "I can't believe they'll be able to save him. The van was in the water for ten minutes before Jill pulled the kids out."

Hawk blew out a breath. "I overheard some of the refugees chattering. I guess the coyotes were helping them until the gators showed up. Then it became every man for himself."

Jill clenched her jaw. "The troopers should've shot the coyotes instead of the gators."

Hawk fiddled with his cell phone, then handed it to Jill. The video captured the roar of the helicopter's engine frothing the water. A second later, the camera panned right, showing Jill swimming toward the van. The scene played out through Jill's rescue of the girl and ended as Hawk reached out to take the child from me.

Jill handed the camera back to Hawk. "Please delete that."

Hawk shook his head. "No way. Unless they see that with their own eyes, nobody will believe that a Yankee woman is crazy enough to dive into a canal full of gators."

Jill blew out a breath. "Fine, email a copy to me, and I'll send it to my mother."

A Florida trooper with sergeant's stripes was talking to Hal Rude, who gestured to us. The sergeant walked over and squatted next to us. "Hal says you two are the Park Service investigators looking into the missing surveyors."

I nodded. "Yeah, we're on temporary assignment from Texas."

He looked at each of us, shaking his head. "Well, I'm sure this chase has nothing to do with your investigation, but I'm sure glad you were here."

There was sudden chattering behind him, and he turned. The boy treated by the Coast Guard crew was coughing and spitting canal water. The sergeant watched for a second, then turned to Jill. "You've had quite a day. He'd be dead if not for you." He pulled two business cards from his pocket and handed one to each of us. "If there is anything the Florida State Patrol can do for you, and I mean *anything,* you call my cell phone."

The trooper started to leave, but Jill waved him back. "These people are Cuban. Why are they running? I thought there was a 'dry feet' policy. If Cubans got ashore, they automatically were granted asylum."

The sergeant squatted and glanced at the wet refugees huddled on the road. The ambulance crew checked their injuries, most having bruises and scrapes from being thrown around in the open van when it ran off the road and hit the water. "That policy ended in 2017. The government decided Cubans were getting an unfair advantage over other immigrants and ended the policy. These poor souls will get an INS hearing. If they have relatives here and a good lawyer, they may be granted asylum."

"And if they aren't?" Jill asked.

The sergeant shrugged. "I'm not sure how Cubans are handled. It's not like Mexico where the US Border Patrol can load a bus with people and drop them off at the border."

We watched him walk back to the other troopers. Hawk looked at the cards we'd been given. "You got yourselves each a 'get out of jail free' card."

Jill was too tired to react. She fingered and read the card. Her head jerked when a helicopter engine started to whine.

"That's the medivac. They're taking the boy from the minivan to St. Pete. He's still unconscious," Hawk said.

I looked at Hawk. "You wouldn't have a Spam sandwich handy, would you?"

"I've got half a dozen in the cooler."

Jill stopped Hawk before he got up. "The Cubans need them worse than Doug."

Hawk trotted to the pickup, and I took Jill's hand. "Are you okay?"

Shrugging, she put the sergeant's card into the pocket of her sodden shorts. "I suppose I might have some nightmares. Seeing those kids floating face down in the back of the van..."

I slid across the grass and pulled her close. "It looks like they're all going to be okay."

"Are we sure there aren't any I didn't find?"

I glanced at the refugees, who were tearing Hawk's sandwiches apart and passing them around. "I think one of the mothers would be screaming if her child was missing."

Jill nodded. "I suppose."

Feeling Jill's holster against my hip, I leaned away. "You didn't take your gun and badge off before you dove in."

"I didn't have time to reason through that." She drew the Glock out of its holster and opened the action, ejecting a cartridge and removing the magazine. Water dripped from the Glock as she picked up the ejected cartridge and fed it back into the magazine. "I suppose I should run a brush through my pistol tonight and put a drop of oil on the slide."

I chuckled. "You should make sure there's not a minnow in the barrel before you fire it."

The tiniest smile crinkled the corners of her mouth. "How can you crack a joke at a time like this?" she asked, reinserting the magazine, working the slide, and putting the Glock back in her holster.

"Gallows humor. You'll learn to use it to cope in situations like this. It's something to look forward to, dear."

# Chapter 8

Tamiami Trail closed for hours as ambulances, helicopters, troopers, and county police investigated the crash, interviewed victims, transported the injured to local hospitals, and the human smugglers to jails. Lines of cars and trucks were backed up for miles, most choosing to turn around rather than wait for the dozens of vehicles with flashing lights to leave.

Hawk drove us back to our cabin in silence.

"Why did alligators approach when the van crashed into the canal?" I asked.

"It's their predatory response to an injured animal falling into the water. Their tiny brains were programmed since they descended from dinosaurs: the first gator to reach a prey animal floundering in the water is the one that eats. The others go hungry."

"They didn't respond to gunfire."

"Those gators probably never had heard a gun discharge, and they don't perceive the sound as a threat."

Jill leaned to the side and looked at Hawk in the rearview mirror. "They've never seen a helicopter before, but that scared them away."

Hawk laughed. "That's a philosophical discussion to be held over a beer."

"You have a theory?"

"Gators are the alpha predator in the Everglades. I suppose a Florida panther might take a baby gator, but for the most part, an adult gator has nothing to fear but humans. Baby gators scatter when the shadow of a bird passes over them. Their brain is programmed, just like the splashing of a prey animal. I think the helicopter represents an enormous predatory bird in their tiny brains."

Jill pondered that. "How tiny a brain are we talking about?"

"Well, I can't say exactly. We sometimes bring in professional hunters to remove problem gators. One of them told me they're aiming at an area smaller than a peach pit."

"Come on," Jill chided. "They're hundreds of pounds, so their brains have to be bigger than a peach pit."

"Nope. The guys said gator brains are smaller than a peach pit. Gators don't think, Jill. They're just eating and breeding machines."

"Holy Hannah!" Jill said. "What would've happened if the helicopter hadn't arrived when it did?"

"I'd prefer not to dwell on that thought." Hawk slowed as he approached the campground turnoff. "Do you guys want to eat? We didn't get lunch."

Jill snorted from the back seat. "I need a shower, and Doug can afford to miss a few meals."

Hawk dropped us near the campground office and got out. "Ma'am, what you did today…"

"I acted on pure adrenaline."

Hawk put out his hand. "That was either the stupidest, craziest, or bravest thing I've ever seen."

"There wasn't any thought that went into the decision, so probably just stupidity."

Hawk smirked. "I seriously doubt that."

We walked the trail back to the cabin as Hawk drove away. "Crap, we didn't make plans for tomorrow," I said.

Jill pulled my arm over her shoulder. "I'm not up for planning right now. Let me take a shower and collapse on the bed."

"We should decide…"

"What part of no plans didn't you understand?"

\* \* \*

The buzzing of my phone jarred me from my concentration on a bass fishing brochure. Fumbling the phone, I didn't look at the caller ID before answering, "Fletcher."

"Douglas, why didn't you send me the video Molly just got?"

"What are you talking about, Mom?"

"Someone named Hawk sent a video of a person swimming in a green pond. The sound is just a roar, so we can't hear any voices. It appears a child is rescued from a submerged van and is handed to you after the rescue. Can you explain why she got it?"

"Jill swam out and rescued two kids out of a van that crashed into a canal. A ranger named Hawk took video of the first rescue."

"This happened while you're on vacation?"

Taking a deep breath, I explained being recalled for a second Florida investigation, the chase, Jill's rescues of the children in the minivan, and her swimming to rescue the kids from the sunken van in the canal.

"What was she thinking?"

"Mom, she reacted to the situation, so not much thinking was involved."

"Why isn't Jill answering Molly's calls?"

"Her phone was in her pocket when she dove into the water. I'm sure it's ruined."

"Tell her to stop doing risky things like that. She could've drowned."

"Mom, she saved the lives of at least two children today."

There was a long pause. "Isn't it someone else's turn?"

"Turn for what?"

"For risking their lives."

The shower water stopped running. "Are you at Al and Molly's ranch?"

"Yes, they invited us over for drinks and supper."

"I'll put Jill on the phone."

I gently knocked on the bathroom door. "You've got a call."

"I'm naked. Take a message."

I opened the door and held out the phone. "It's Mother."

I went back to the brochure advertising guided backwater fishing trips with a guarantee that guests would catch at least an eight-pound bass, or the trip would be free. I'd never seen a four-pound bass, so the fat bass on the front of the brochure looked like a new species to me.

Jill stepped out of the bathroom wrapped in a towel. She looked unhappy and handed the phone to me. "Your turn. It's my mother."

"Hi, Molly."

"Douglas Fletcher, you promised to love and protect my daughter when you married her. What in hell were you thinking?" Molly Rickowski sounded as angry as I'd ever heard her.

"I wasn't there."

136

"You were there! Jill handed that little girl to you."

"I wasn't there when she dove into the canal and swam to the van where the kids were trapped." I paused. "Molly, she saved two lives today."

"I know that! Why didn't you swim out to help her?"

"I…um…didn't think of it."

"Damn you! Take care of her, will you? I expect both of you back here for Thanksgiving, intact and healthy. Do you understand me?" I doubted we'd get away for Thanksgiving, but this wasn't the moment to point that out. "Got it."

"Put Jill back on."

I held out the phone, but Jill shook her head as she pulled on a fresh t-shirt. "She's tied up right now. I'll have her call you when she gets free."

"Do you know what we do to ornery bulls who don't perform as expected?" Molly asked.

"No."

"We send them to the slaughterhouse to be made into sausage. Do you get my drift?"

"Yes, Mom."

I ended the call and threw the phone on the bed. "Even Florida isn't far enough away from our families."

Jill carried her wet clothes into the bathroom and ran the shower over them. "Cell phones make the world a small place."

"We need to call Matt and let him know what happened today." When Jill didn't respond, I walked into the bathroom. "Would you like me to call Mandy instead?"

Jill stared at the water running over her clothes. "Do we have to call anyone?"

"I'm afraid so. Hawk's boss, Chad, sent the video to the television station. We need to let Matt know before he hears about it from someone else."

Jill nodded without speaking. I dialed Mattson's home phone, and Mandy answered on the second ring. "Mandy, I've got a very rattled wife who needs to talk to you."

"Oh, Doug, what happened?"

I held out the phone to Jill, who reluctantly accepted it. I closed the bathroom door and walked to the campground office.

The office permeated with the aroma of tomatoes and spices coming from Jubal's apartment in the rear of the office building. Looking up from a small television in the campground office, Jubal turned his head. "Help you?"

"I don't suppose you do room service?"

Jubal cackled and nodded toward two vending machines. "I suppose I could deliver a couple cans of soda and chips, but I'd expect a mighty fine tip."

Looking me over, he paused. "You've been rolling in the dirt?"

"We had an incident on the road."

"I heard the trail was closed for several hours. That was something you did?"

"A van ran off the road and crashed into the canal."

"I heard the sirens go past, and then people started coming in saying the road was closed. I heard some helicopters, too. Your partner looked like she went swimming in a pond."

"Something like that."

"Hang on." Jubal turned the television off and disappeared into the back room. He returned with two sweaty cans of beer and handed one to me, gesturing toward two chairs near the front door. "I was a bartender in a previous life. Talk to me."

I told him about the chase, crash, and Jill's swim.

"Whooee! You two had yourselves quite a day!"

"Jill's pretty messed up. She's talking to a Texas friend, and I'm letting her process what happened."

"And you don't want to be around a bunch of people in a restaurant right now."

"Probably not."

Nodding, Jubal sat quietly for a moment. "Hang on. I might have an answer for you."

I waited and finished off my beer. I expected Jubal to return with a menu from an Everglades City pizza delivery place, but instead, he showed up with a small pot and a paper bag. He held them out to me. "Here's your room service."

"I can't eat your supper."

"Mr. Fletcher, we made a big pot of gumbo. If you don't eat this bit of it, we'll have leftovers for days."

My movement toward my wallet made Jubal frown. "Don't insult me by offering to pay. This is a gift." I accepted the bag and pot. "Leave the pot and utensils on the table, and I'll pick them up tomorrow when I bring fresh towels."

"Thank you."

"Sir, it's entirely my pleasure."

Jill was sitting at the table when I walked in. Looking up from her concentrated stare at a drop of condensation rolling down the side of a water bottle. "What's that?" She nodded toward the pot and brown bag.

"Jubal sent gumbo for our supper."

Jill frowned. "You went begging for food?"

Setting down the pot and opening the bag, I replied, "He demanded that I take what he described as future leftovers."

I handed Jill a beer, then set two spoons and a plastic-wrapped tube of crackers on the table. "Are there any bowls in there?"

I pulled a chair next to her and handed her a spoon. "Eating right out of the pot is like being back in college."

The comment made Jill smile. "I don't remember eating out of a saucepan when I was in college. Maybe South Dakota coeds are more civilized than Minnesota boys."

I lifted the lid off the pot, filling the room with the aromatic gumbo. "I didn't carry a pistol to school. Tell me who was more civilized." I stirred the tomato, rice, okra, and shrimp mixture.

Blowing on a spoonful of steaming gumbo, Jill shook her head. "You overcame that gun-toting shortcoming when you got a job as a cop."

The first bite of gumbo set my mouth on fire, so I stripped the wrapper off the crackers and popped two into my mouth with no effect on the pepper burn. Jill watched with amusement.

We ate quietly and talked about the gumbo, the swamp noises outside, the heat, the humidity—anything unrelated to the day's events. Jill blew on another spoonful of gumbo. "Talking to Mandy helped."

"What did she say?"

"I don't know if it's what she says as much as her cool reassuring voice. She's always upbeat and supportive."

"Is she going to tell Matt, so he's not blindsided?"

"Mandy handed the phone to Matt."

"And?"

"And I told him what happened."

"Did you warn him about the video?"

Jill shook her head and stared at her spoonful of gumbo.

Picking up the phone, I found the video and forwarded it to Matt.

"What are you doing?"

"I sent Matt the video before it shows up from another source."

"I'm not recognizable, right?"

"You're a dot swimming through the water until you hand the girl to me. Mom didn't recognize you, the algae-covered drowned rat in the video."

"Good. Mom said she tried to call me, so I guess my phone drowned during the swim."

"I saw a strip mall in Everglades City with a cell phone shop. We can stop there when we go to the surveyors' office tomorrow."

"I want to go to the St. Pete hospital tomorrow."

"To check on the boy?"

She nodded.

"What if…?"

"Then, I'll want to talk to his mother."

"They might not want to talk to us."

"I need closure."

I set down my spoon and took her hand. "Cops don't often get closure. Accident victims get treated and released. HIPAA laws prevent hospital personnel from updating you on victims. Criminals have charges dropped or plea-bargained down. Detectives investigate and close cases without talking to the arresting officers. It's just a fact of the job."

She spun the wedding ring on my finger. "Leave the rental car and ride with Hawk tomorrow. I'll go by myself if you don't want to come along."

"It's not that I don't want to go. I don't want you hurt by something out of our control." I paused. "The news we get as cops is usually...unpleasant."

We were startled by a knock on the cabin door. I reached for my pistol as Jill walked to the door. She cracked the door open an inch against the security chain, then immediately released the chain and pulled it open.

Hal Rude's silhouette made him and his wife nearly invisible against the background of the swamp. "I hope I'm not intruding, but I thought you might require a beer."

I stood, expecting Hal to walk in with a six-pack of beer. Instead, a beautiful woman wearing a summery dress swept into the room with a bottle of wine in each hand, and Hal followed with a 24-pack of beer.

The woman pecked Jill's cheek and held out the wine bottles. "Hal thinks everyone in the world likes cold beer. I figured you might not have a corkscrew, so we bought screw-cap bottles." She paused. "I'm sorry, Hal's told me so much about you. I feel like we're already friends. I'm Trish."

Jill smiled but was unprepared for the sudden onslaught of energy Trish brought into the room. "Um, I think we've only got a couple plastic glasses."

Trish's smile was disarming. "Honey, we can drink this straight from the bottle if we have to."

Hal set the cardboard beer carton on the table and tore it open. He handed me a beer. "Unlike my wife, I don't assume every woman would rather drink wine than beer." He held out a sweating can of beer to Jill.

"Actually, I'll have a plastic cup of white wine with Trish."

I touched my can to Hal's. "How did you find us?"

"I'm a cop and know how to find people." Hal waited until Jill and Trish were dealing with the wine, then he leaned close. "I spoke with Jubal. Anyone who calls will be told you checked out this afternoon."

"Is that necessary?" Then I paused. "Shit. The video is out?"

"Several videos are making the rounds. The one from the Coast Guard helicopter, dashcam video from our cars, a couple carloads of tourists were taking video. Each local channel has its own video. Some are saying unidentified good Samaritans jumped into action. Others identify Jill as a Park Service ranger. One has both your full names. I expect they'll all have it right by morning."

"Do you know how the kid from the minivan is doing?"

"He's conscious, being held overnight for observation."

"No spinal injuries because he got pulled out of the vehicle without a backboard or neck brace?"

"No one's mentioned any injuries except a concussion." Hal paused. "The Cuban kids are okay, too."

"Please tell Jill. She's worried."

Hal shook his head as Trish and Jill walked to the table with their glasses and the open wine bottle. "Not tonight."

Trish had her arm around Jill's waist and said, "So, Hal Junior sees us going out the door, and I can see he's planning something. I looked him in the eye and said, 'no girls.' He gets all defensive like he doesn't know what I'm talking about, but I know he's thinking about inviting Myah over as soon as we walk out the door."

"How will you know if she comes over?"

Trish pulled a cell phone out of her bra and touched the screen. "Here's the view from our Ring doorbell. I'll know whoever comes through the door."

Hal leaned toward me. "Like he doesn't know how to sneak her in through a window."

"Jill, tell them what happened to you when you tried sneaking in through the bedroom window."

Jill rolled her eyes. "I got sprayed by a skunk when I snuck behind the house in the dark. Mom dragged me under the porch light and poured tomato juice over my head while a half dozen cowboys watched from the bunkhouse."

Trish threw her head back and laughed like she'd never heard anything so funny. "Oh lord, that's what I call divine justice. Have you done that to any of your kids?"

"Doug and I have only been married a little over a year. No kids."

Hal shook his head. "I love my kids dearly, but their teen years have been a trial. I understand why lions sometimes eat their young."

Trish pushed his shoulder. "Don't say things like that! People might believe you."

We talked, comparing growing up in the Midwest vs. south Florida. In no time at all,

146

the first bottle of wine was gone, and it was nearly ten o'clock. Trish stood up and hugged Jill. "If you need anything while you're here, you call. Understand?"

"I can't imagine what we'd need."

"Honey, call about anything. A home-cooked meal, a friend who'll understand that you need to complain about your husband, anything."

Jill held my hand as we watched Hal and Trish disappear into the darkness. "Did you know they were going to visit tonight?"

"No, but I'm glad they did. I don't think you would've been very entertaining tonight if not for them. Hal said the boy from the minivan is conscious and is being held overnight for observation. He'll probably be released before we can get to the hospital."

"I'm going to have nightmares."

Hugging her close, I said, "You'd be a sociopath if you didn't."

"Sociopaths don't have nightmares?"

"Those are just dreams for sociopaths, and they don't find them disturbing."

# Chapter 9

Walking out of the bathroom wrapped in a towel, I was surprised to see Hawk sitting with Jill at the table. There were four Styrofoam cups on the table with sugar and cream packets. Jill's hair was damp, and she was dressed in shorts and a golf shirt.

Hawk glanced at me. "Sorry to interrupt your shower."

"You should be relieved that I wrapped myself in a towel before I walked out of the bathroom."

The corner of Hawk's mouth twitched. "Yeah, that would be one of those moments I'd have to try to erase from my memory."

I pulled clothes out of the suitcase, then paused. "Are we going into Everglades City or slogging through the swamps today?"

"It's up to you guys. You wanted to talk to the surveyors' office manager, so that means we'll go into town first."

I glanced at the sodden shoes Jill and I had worn the day before, then at the flip-flops Jill wore. "I don't suppose our shoes will dry out if we leave them in our cabin for the day."

Hawk considered my comments while staring at the shoes. "The only way you'll dry them in this humidity is to put them into an oven or a laundromat dryer."

"Jill needs a new cell phone, and we could buy some new shoes if we go to Everglades City."

Hawk clenched his jaw and then let out a sigh. "If we spend the day shoe shopping and interviewing the office manager, that's another day lost from our search for the surveyors."

I took clothes out and hung them over my arm. "There's a trade-off in our decision. We can randomly race from place to place, hoping we'll find the survey crew. Or we can get smarter and maybe find the right places to look for them."

Jill wrinkled her nose. "It's hard to take you seriously while you're naked. Let's finish this discussion when you're presentable, maybe over breakfast."

I paused. "I'm sorry, Hawk. I don't mean to bulldoze you. If you've got some spots that you think are likely places to search for the surveyors, we'll gladly go with you and help search."

Hawk shook his head. "Nah, I've got nothing particular in mind. I think your suggestion to step back and plan, rather than just aimlessly ramming around, is pretty good."

I slipped into the bathroom with my clothes and heard the murmur of Hawk and Jill's voices. They were still at the table when I came out, and their smiles told me I was the butt of some joke.

"What?"

Jill picked up two coffee cups and handed one to me. "Hawk was concerned that you'd missed a meal yesterday and definitely needed breakfast before we dove into our other plans."

"And you disagreed?"

"Not at all. I'm ready for breakfast, too. Last night's gumbo is gone."

Hawk held the door, still smiling. "Jill said missing your usual greasy breakfast for a month would probably lower your cholesterol."

"I have it on good authority that my cholesterol has nothing to do with the consumption of greasy breakfasts."

Jill glanced over her shoulder at me. "Whose good authority would that be?"

"Your mother."

Jill turned. "You're citing my chubby mother as your health consultant?"

"She said she liked feeding me because I appreciated her cooking."

Hawk shook his head at our banter as we walked to the pickup. I got in the back, and after starting the engine, he leaned on the seatback. "I told Jill that the kids from the minivan are fine. The boy is being released from the hospital this morning. The Cuban boy from the van still is hospitalized. He'd been under water a long time when Jill got to him. He's breathing, but the doctors are concerned he may have suffered brain damage from oxygen deprivation."

Hawk drove west toward Everglades City and parked on the street. The city was quiet except for the people going in and out of a small café. In addition to our vehicle, there were half a dozen pickups loaded with ladders or gear, the working people eating breakfast before starting their workday.

Waiting inside the door, a waitress nodded to us, then hustled over to clear the dishes from a booth.

"This place looks newer than the town," Jill said, looking around at the people inside the café.

"The Hurricane Irma storm surge inundated Everglades City. The buildings survived, but nearly every house and business ended up filled with muddy, bacteria-laden water. A major cleanup was required, and this place was gutted and rebuilt."

The waitress nodded to us, and we threaded our way through the tables to the freshly cleaned booth. "Coffee?" asked the middle-aged waitress as she handed us plastic laminated menus.

We all nodded, and Jill said, "Black, please."

"We live in Port Aransas, Texas," Jill said as she perused the menu. "Hurricane Harvey flattened the Corpus Christi area two months before Irma hit here. Houses and businesses still are boarded up that haven't been able to rebuild."

Hawk set his menu on the table. "That's the risk of living near the coast. The mayor is touting this area as hurricane safe because, on average, we're hit every ten to twenty years."

Shaking my head, I set my menu down. "I suppose he needs to say that to attract investors, but the hurricanes don't really pay attention to averages and odds."

With a nametag that read Dottie, our waitress swept back with three mugs and a coffee pot. She set out the mugs and, as she poured, asked, "Y'all ready to order?"

Hawk gestured for Jill to order first. "I'll have oatmeal and a bowl of fruit."

Dottie set the coffee pot down and took out a pen and an order pad. "Oatmeal, not grits?"

Smiling, Jill nodded. "I've never developed a taste for grits."

"Hap makes 'em with butter, and we've got ham gravy."

"Just boring oatmeal for me," Jill replied.

152

Hawk gathered the menus. "I'll have grits and gravy, Dottie."

Dottie sized me up. "You look like a biscuit and gravy man."

"That sounds good."

Writing our orders, Dottie added, "The biscuits and gravy are today's special. Coffee is included."

"Great," I said as Hawk handed the menus to Dottie.

I looked around the room at the mix of customers. They were nearly all male, many with worn baseball caps and most looking like they worked hard for a living. "This looks like the place the locals choose for meals."

Hawk nodded. "This doesn't have the glitzy tourist appeal, and they serve tasty comfort food at good prices. The tourists are drawn to places out of town with neon signs. No drinks with little umbrellas served here." He paused and looked around to see if anyone was listening to us. "What do you hope to find at the surveyors' office?"

"You talked to them and got the location where we found the blood. I hope we can determine where else those surveyors had been working recently and ask if they'd had confrontations with the protesters or anyone else."

"Like I said, the office person I spoke with was disorganized and had to search through handwritten notes to determine where the surveyors had been. I don't think he was involved in scheduling or dispatching the survey crews."

"The surveyors' office didn't report them missing," Jill asked.

Hawk shook his head. "The female surveyor's ex-husband called the Florida City police when she didn't pick up her children from him at the appointed time. The office manager reported them missing later that day."

Digesting that, Jill nodded. "The guy in the office might know something more if we ask the right questions."

Breakfast arrived before Hawk could field more questions. The plate Dottie set in front of me had gravy dripping off one edge. Four biscuits were swimming in gravy dotted with a half-pound of sausage lumps. Jill looked resigned at my choice as Dottie set a bowl of oatmeal in front of her with sides of brown sugar, butter, raisins, and cream. Her fruit plate was fresh grapefruit and orange sections heaped in a large bowl. Hawk's grits came with a small pitcher of white gravy.

Dottie stepped back and surveyed the table. "I'll refill your coffee in a second. Is there anything else I can grab for you?"

"This looks great," Jill replied. "I don't need anything more."

Stirring butter, raisins, and brown sugar into her oatmeal, Jill nodded toward my plate. "That's about twice the amount of biscuits and gravy my mother served you. Can you eat that much?"

I spread a napkin on my lap. "I'll give it my best effort."

Hawk listened to our banter as he poured gravy over his grits. "How long have you two been married?"

"A little over a year," I replied. I took a bite of biscuit and must've made a happy sound because Jill looked up as she speared a grapefruit section.

"The biscuits are good?"

I cut off a piece and held it out to her. "You have to try this."

Jill ate the biscuit off my fork, and her eyes lit up. "I've never had biscuits this light and crumbly. I don't know how they get them out of the pan without them falling to pieces."

Hawk pushed his bowl toward Jill. "The grits are just as good as the biscuits. You don't know what you're missing."

Jill reached out with her spoon and scooped a bit of grits out of Hawk's bowl. She tasted them tentatively, then chuckled. "Those are really good grits, but I'm still an oatmeal girl."

Dottie swept through, topping off coffee mugs and checking on her customers. "Everything still tasting good?" We all nodded, then she looked at Jill's untouched cream pitcher. "Honey, try some of that cream on your oatmeal. You could use some meat on your bones."

Jill was about to answer, but Dottie was already gone. "She sounds like my mother."

Hawk finished his grits and wiped his mouth. "Dottie is everyone's mother and serves food, news, and advice."

Jill poured a dribble of cream on the oatmeal and stirred. "This is how my mom used to serve it when I was growing up, my style of comfort food."

Dottie was back with more coffee before we'd had more than a sip. She smiled when she picked up Hawk's empty bowl. "Looks like the grits were a hit with you."

"My friends need shoes, Dottie. Where's the best place in town to get them?"

"The tourists all go to the big discount mall in Naples." She paused. "We locals go to the Everglades Fishing Company. The price is a little higher, but we like to support the local economy."

Jill pushed her empty fruit bowl to Dottie. "That sounds like a bait shop."

Dottie set our bill on the table and picked up Jill's bowl. "Honey, you can get anything from ghost shrimp to groceries there. If you need a pair of shoes, they'll have 'em."

Jill blew out a breath and pushed her still half-full bowl of oatmeal away. "I suppose we'll have to kill time until they open."

Hawk laughed. "They're a bait shop and open at sunrise before the early boats go out."

I grabbed the bill and left Dottie a generous tip. Hawk led us to the pickup. "Thanks for breakfast."

Jill climbed in the back seat. "Thanks for introducing us to that great café. What a treat."

The Everglades Fishing Company was only a few blocks away, and the parking lot was nearly full, even early in the morning. The store was huge, well-lit, and, as billed, had coolers of food across from a selection of fishing rods and tackle. We walked to the rear of the store. Hawk explored fishing tackle as Jill and I looked at the footwear.

"Dottie's right," Jill said as she looked at the selection of women's shoes and boots. "The prices aren't bargain basement, but they're fair, and the selection is good."

I chose a pair of hiking boots and a package of socks while Jill tried on a variety of shoes with the help of a young man. Hawk found me standing on the edge of the clothing section with my shoebox and socks. "Jill's not as quick as you?"

I shook my head. "Let's hope this is quicker than the bathing suit shopping trip."

Jill came down the aisle with two shoe boxes, clothing draped over her arm, and

157

other items in her hands. "Here, take the shoe boxes. I want to get a couple long-sleeve UPF shirts."

"We have clothes back at the cabin."

Jill handed me her selections. "I think everything I wore on yesterday's swim is ruined, and I don't have enough clothes for days of trekking through the swamp."

"We're going to need another suitcase," I muttered.

Jill had taken two steps away but stopped when she heard my complaint. "Good idea. I'm sure they have suitcases."

Hawk and I watched Jill walk toward a rack of sun visors with the EFC logo. He leaned close. "I'll get a shopping cart, so you don't have to carry all that stuff in your arms."

Jill told the checkout clerk to skip the bags. "Just load all the clothing into the suitcase." She looked at me. "Get out your VISA card."

"My VISA card?"

She paused. "Right. Our VISA card."

I pulled out my wallet and prepared to slip the card into the reader as the total on the cash register passed $400.

Hawk leaned close. "You haven't been married all that long, but you are catching on. I've seen too many guys argue about a shopping bill. You can't win. Best just to suck it up and pay."

The clerk scanned the last item, a long-sleeve shirt with a 50-UPF tag. The total jumped another $79.99, and I grimaced but bit my tongue as I slipped the card into the reader.

"Would you like me to cut off the tags?" asked the young female clerk.

Jill nodded. "That'd be great. I'm going to change in your restroom."

Hawk and I waited in the pickup while Jill changed. Smiling, he glanced at the door. "This is probably the best therapy for Jill today. It's got her focused on moving ahead from yesterday's mess. Her new, clean clothes are symbolic of a fresh start."

"Hawk, you're wise beyond your years."

Jill walked out of the store, dressed in an entirely new outfit, her old clothes in a plastic shopping bag. "I've dealt with some people who suffered from PTSD. Each of them dealt with it in a different way, but they all needed to make physical changes to help them move ahead."

I watched as Jill walked across the parking lot, and she smiled and had a spark that hadn't been there earlier. "I hope this is enough to help her move on."

Hawk shook his head. "This is a short-term fix, but it's a start."

Jill set her bag of old clothes on the floor and buckled her seat belt. "How far are we from the surveyors' office?"

Hawk started the engine. "Nothing in Everglades City is more than a five-minute drive away."

"You should take your damp shoes out of the bag, so they don't soak everything else," I said.

"My damp shoes were soggy and had soaked my socks. They're in the restroom garbage can with my socks."

Hawk smiled as he pulled out of the parking lot. "Seems like a good choice to me. They weren't going to dry in this humidity."

"Oh, before I forget, stop at the cell phone store."

Hawk nodded. "Yeah, there's one in the strip mall next to the surveyors' office."

We parked in an open spot just as the store manager lit the OPEN sign. "I'll just be a minute," Jill said as she opened the pickup door.

With Jill gone, I looked at Hawk. "Her minutes tend to be a little long."

"You told me about swimsuit shopping."

"I have a Navajo colleague in Arizona. I wonder if growing up on an Everglades reservation is different from his experience in the desert."

Hawk laughed. "You mean, besides being surrounded by water vs. living in the desert?"

"I was wondering about the difference between your cultures."

Hawk leaned back. "Well, it depends on how far back you want to look. The Miccosukee was one of the eight aboriginal tribes living in Florida before the arrival of the Spaniards. Legend says we lived in peace with our neighbors, hunting, fishing, and raising corn."

"And then the Spaniards and English showed up, and everything went to hell."

"Pretty much. Many of the tribes had become entirely wiped out in the Creek War of 1813 and the first Seminole war. The Southern Creek tribe ceded their lands in Alabama, Florida, and Georgia and relocated to Oklahoma. The rest of the tribes lived an uneasy existence, being pushed off the coastal and good farming lands by encroaching White settlers. In 1823, the Moultrie treaty guaranteed peace for 20 years, moving the remaining indigenous people to a central Florida reservation. Then, the Indian Removal Act was signed in 1830, and the government decided to round up the central Florida tribes and move them to less desirable land in the west. That led to the Second and Third Seminole wars that ended in 1855.

"The Miccosukee retreated to the Everglades and adapted to life on the hammocks, hunting, fishing, and eating the native plants. The construction of the Tamiami Trail in 1928 brought a flood of Whites to the area. The Everglades

National Park was established, which pushed us north. When the government officially recognized the Miccosukee tribe in 1958, there were only 550 tribal members. The reservation was established in 1962, and all of the current tribal members descended from that group of survivors."

"Is the tribe prospering?"

"I guess we're doing well. We have a constitution, a school, a clinic, a general store, a restaurant, a gas station, and some oil leases. We're not getting rich, but there are jobs, and people are generally happy."

"We went past the town when we drove from Florida City to Everglades City on the Tamiami Trail."

"Yeah, it's just past the east end of the Big Cypress Preserve loop road. You should stop by and check it out if you have time. There's a cultural center and airboat rides."

Jill exited the store smiling with a bag in her hand. "You guys won't believe what these new phones can do."

Hawk backed out of the parking spot, and I interrupted Jill. "Show me after we talk to the surveyors' office manager."

# Chapter 10

The surveyors' office, a small building past a strip mall off the corner of Tamiami Trail and Thomason Road, was tucked behind a bank, nearly hidden from view. The only identification was the address stenciled above the door and the name, "Naples Surveying," in small letters on the door. Naples Surveying didn't cater to attracting walk-in business.

A buzzer sounded when I opened the door, and cool air and the smell of paper hit us. The small office had three desks with computers and monitors against the walls, all stacked with files and maps. A printer in the back corner was big enough to print a 36" wide map, probably a necessity for surveyors. File cabinets lined the left wall, some large enough to accommodate a sizable flat map.

A young man sat at a desk in the back corner and looked up over the top of his computer monitor. "Can I help y'all?"

We must've been backlit by the open door with only our silhouettes visible. The young man jumped up when the door closed, apparently reacting to Hawk's uniform, the badges on our belts, and the pistols on our hips. "We'd like to talk to someone about the surveys your missing crew were working on."

"Um, sure. What would you like to know?"

Signaling our intention to stay until we got answers, Jill sat in the chair nearest the office guy's desk. "We know they were marking drilling leases on National Park Service land when they disappeared. Did they mention any friction with the protesters?"

Sensing his lapse in propriety, our host offered his hand to Jill. "I'm sorry. I'm Paul Lawler, Mike's son." Then turned to Hawk and me, shaking hands and pulling over other office chairs. "You haven't found my dad."

I sat and tried to be evasive but sound supportive and hopeful. The mental image of brain matter splattered on the grass came to me, and I had to shake it off. "Not yet. We're still gathering information. Were the protesters harassing your dad and Terri?"

"He didn't mention it, but I really don't know. Dad and Terri worked in the field, and I only saw them a couple times a week when they came in to get maps or leave marked-up maps to update on the computer. Dad never said anything about problems with the protesters. Terri said they'd seen protesters, but the focus of the protests was the drilling sites. No one seemed to care much about the survey truck. I suppose media coverage of protesters with a drilling rig in the background is more compelling than the video of a couple surveyors slogging through a swamp."

Jill leaned forward. "Did they mention threatening phone calls, emails, or letters?"

Paul paused in thought. "Their cell phone numbers weren't published, so if there had been threats, they would've come here, to the office. I handle the business email and open the office mail. I haven't seen anything threatening regarding the oil lease surveys."

"Have you received any emails or texts?" I asked.

Paul shook his head. "Like I said, the drilling protesters didn't seem to care about us."

Jill straightened up. Something Paul said had piqued her interest. "There haven't been any threats about the oil surveys, but you paused. Have there been other threats?"

"I wouldn't call them threats as much as complaints."

"Who's been complaining?" I asked.

"An old orchard is up for sale, and the owners contracted with us to do a survey.

There's a developer ready to buy the property, and the buyer wants to know the property boundaries. I guess he's designing a golf course and wants to locate all the high ground. I think the state requires that he maintain the wetlands, so he's trying to find every inch of high ground on the orchard property."

"Was that a problem?"

"There wasn't really a problem with the orchard, but the neighbors were unhappy because they've been grazing cattle on a piece of land they'd fenced and in error, thought was theirs."

Jill frowned. "So, your dad and Terri were confronted by the angry neighbor?"

"Naw, they never saw anyone when they were marking the property boundaries. The guy called the office when he saw the survey stakes in the pasture. He chewed my butt and told me to keep off his property. I explained that we were just marking the property lines defined in the property abstracts. I told him to call the county if he thought there was a problem with the property lines."

Jill glanced at me, then back to Paul. "Can you show us the properties on a map?"

"I just scanned the map into the computer, so the paper map is right here." He picked up a plat drawing and carried it to the desk behind Jill. We stood next to him as he spread the map on the desktop and pointed out the landmarks to us. "Here's the Tamiami Trail, and the orchard is just north of the roadway and west of the National Preserve. A whole section of the orchard is being developed." Paul ran his finger over the boundaries of the orchard, then outlined a bottom corner with a red pencil. "This forty-acre parcel abuts the cattle ranch but is part of the orchard parcel."

Jill placed her finger in the center of the smaller red square. "So, this is the disputed forty-acre tract. What's a forty-acre parcel of agricultural land cost?"

Paul stepped back and blew out his breath. "It depends on the land. The orchard is listed for $3,500,000, and about a third of it is a swamp. I suppose a dry forty like this would probably sell for upwards of $250,000."

Jill traced the orchard with her finger. "What's the adjoining land like?"

"The western part is a mix of hardwood hammocks and swamp until you get to the eastern part abutting the national preserve. That's an orchard."

I pointed to the land south of the orchard. "Who owns this tract?"

"That's Butch Conley's place, the one who called with a burr under his blanket about the survey stakes."

"A quarter-million is a pretty big burr," Jill said, straightening up.

"Do you think Butch wants to buy it?" I asked.

Paul shook his head. "Butch is probably like most of the ranchers, land rich but cash poor. He's sitting on a couple million dollars of pasture but has to sell cattle to pay his taxes."

Jill drew a deep breath. "Western South Dakota and eastern Wyoming are like that, too. Losing forty acres of pasture is a big deal."

Paul ran his finger over the land, next to the orchard property. "This is Butch's place, and all these little symbols show the swampy land. That forty acres is probably a quarter of his dry pasture. So yes, losing that acreage is a big deal to Butch."

"So, most of his land is swampy and unusable?" Jill asked.

"Most of the swampy areas are wet in the summer and dry in the winter."

"Do Butch and the orchard owner get along?" Jill asked.

"Oh, hell no. Butch and his neighbors are always at it about something. I swear Butch would argue that black was white just to be ornery."

"Did he threaten you when he called?"

"He ranted and swore. If he thought the property lines were wrong, I told him to take it up with the county. I explained that all we did was put survey stakes on the property lines defined by the legal property description."

"And he accepted that?" I asked.

Paul shook his head. "He told me to shove my stakes where the sun doesn't shine."

"What did you say?"

"I told him to have a nice day and hung up."

"How long ago was that?"

Paul walked to his desk and pulled up a calendar on his computer. "Dad surveyed the orchard last Tuesday. I think Butch called on Thursday."

Jill studied the calendar and put her finger on the following Monday. "This is when your dad and Terri disappeared?"

"Yeah, they weren't here when I locked up Monday night. My mom called after supper and asked if I knew where dad was. I called his cell and the office and didn't get an answer on either phone. I drove back here and checked the office, and nobody had been here."

"Did you report them missing Monday night?" I asked.

"I called the dispatcher, and she said they'd keep an eye out for the truck. I thought maybe they'd got stuck somewhere out of cell phone range. Tuesday morning, I called back and made an official missing person's report. By then, Terri's ex had already reported her missing."

Jill shook her head. "Are there any areas out of cell phone range where they'd be working?"

Paul shook his head. "Not many, but there are some."

"Do they usually return to the office at the end of every day?"

"No. They have all their gear in the truck, and most nights, Dad just drops Terri off at her house. They only come into the office a couple times a week to pick up and drop off maps. If anything comes up in between, I call Dad's cell phone."

"Did you tell him about Butch's call?"

"We joked about it when Dad called in. He said he wouldn't want to be in the county assessor's office when Butch came to complain about the property lines."

Jill cocked her head. "He wasn't concerned but was he planning to drive over and smooth things over with Butch?"

Paul looked at each of us. "There wasn't much point in doing that. Butch was hot and talking to him would only stir things up. Besides, the orchard owner requested the survey, and he was our customer, not Butch."

Jill looked at me and raised her eyebrows. "I guess we should talk to Butch Conley and the orchard owner."

Paul went to his desk and peeled off a Post-it note. "You probably want to talk to Conrad Polk, the developer. Hector Sanchez, the orchard owner, lives in Tampa. I've got to warn you. Butch isn't a pleasant man."

I walked next to Hawk as we returned to the truck. "Do you know Butch Conley?"

"Only by reputation. He doesn't have anything to do with the Park Service except when his cattle wander off during the dry season. He rounds them up, and we don't see him."

Jill got in the front seat. "Is the orchard development controversial?"

"Mostly from a wetlands perspective and the traffic that it'll bring on some back roads. There are folks with their noses out of joint over both those issues."

"Are they angry enough to kill someone?"

"I don't think any sane person would kill over traffic on a back road, and neither of those issues has anything to do with the surveyors."

Hawk pulled onto the road and turned north on the highway. "So, what did we learn?"

"The surveyors pissed off Butch Conley," I said. "But Butch never physically confronted them, and it sounds like his complaint is with the county and the developer."

"So, what are we doing now?"

"I'd like to visit the house the protesters are renting," I said. "I wonder if they're really as harmless as they'd like us to believe." I looked at Hawk in the mirror. "What do you think?"

"The protesters are certainly worth a look." He smiled at Jill. "You might want to wear your new boots. You won't find a picture of their house in *Better Homes and Gardens* or *Good Housekeeping*."

Jill looked unsettled. "Why are we talking to the protesters and not the angry rancher? He's a hothead and seems like someone more likely to fly off the handle than the protesters who seem indifferent to the surveys."

"They both deserve a look," I said. "But sometimes, the best alibi is feigned indifference. The protesters are unhappy about the drilling, and everything associated with it, but they seem to ignore the surveyors, who lay the groundwork for the drilling. It seems too...convenient for them to be against the drilling but not show their contempt for the surveys."

Hawk glanced at Jill in the mirror. "Besides, I feel a lot less anxious about going to the protesters' compound than knocking on a local hothead's door. It'd be better if we got him away from his house."

Jill considered Hawk's comments. "What you're really saying is catching him away from his guns."

"He'll probably have a gun wherever you confront him. I don't want to walk up to a door not knowing if there's a shotgun pointed at me from the other side."

"And that's not a problem where the protesters are staying?"

"Based on my experience, the biggest risks at the protesters' house are the cockroaches and getting cooties from hippie women who don't shave their legs or armpits."

"Really, Hawk? I don't expect we'll get close enough to the 'hippie women' to catch cooties from them."

"I'm no cootie expert," Hawk said, "But if they're half as aggressive as the roaches..."

Jill realized her chain was being yanked, and she backed down. "Sounds like I'll need to wear my boots into their house."

Hawk nodded emphatically. "You may also want to shower after we leave to get the odor of marijuana smoke out of your hair."

We turned off the Tamiami Trail onto a rutted driveway. "Isn't this National Park Service property?"

173

"Yeah, they're staying in an old house on the land donated to the government. There's some clause in the property donation that allowed the house to remain as long as the ownership stayed in the family and the property is occupied. When the family decided the property was too run down to maintain, the ownership transferred to the Park Service."

Jill unbuckled her seat belt and leaned forward. "Why haven't the protesters been evicted?"

"I've put up a barricade at the entrance, but it disappears. Chad and I agreed that doing more than that would stir them up and cause public relations issues for the preserve, so we decided to leave them alone as long as they're not doing damage."

The two-story house was in extreme disrepair. It had once featured white clapboard siding, but most of the paint had peeled off the graying wood. Blue tarps were nailed to the roof, reflecting the state of the few cedar shingles visible between them. Several windows had broken glass with the openings covered from the inside with soggy cardboard. An outhouse, with its door ajar, sat thirty yards behind the house, near the fringe of brush and trees. A trail through the tall grass was beaten from the house's side door to the leaning outhouse. A five-gallon, black plastic pail hung from a tree branch, and a pipe ran to a showerhead.

"I love their solar-heated shower," Jill said.

"No shower curtain," I observed.

Hawk chuckled. "The first time I drove in here, one of the women was showering in the yard. I expected her to cover up with a towel or turn away, but she waved, like her standing there naked was no big thing."

"Ahh," Jill said. "That's where your comment about the hippie women with unshaved armpits came from."

Hawk was about to say more but hesitated. "Yes."

Two cars were parked near the back door. One was an old Toyota with oxidized blue paint, the other a Volkswagen minivan that looked like it had once been converted into an RV camper. Smoke rose lazily from a steel drum behind the house, and its smoky haze smelled of burned food and plastic. A pile of plastic garbage bags near the back door was spilling bottles, aluminum cans, and soup cans.

Jill tapped my shoulder. "I would expect environmental activists to be recycling food containers rather than burning them."

Hawk parked next to the minivan. "I expect they recycle some stuff, but there's a trade-off between burning gas to haul your recyclables to Sweetwater and burning the plastics."

Jill unlatched the back door. "Their credibility as eco-protesters just dropped."

Hawk led us to the screen door on the side of the house. I could hear voices inside as he knocked. "Hello, it's your local ranger here to visit."

I heard chairs scraping on the wooden floor and muffled voices. "Hang on a second."

Jill sniffed the air. "I think they're using a marijuana scented air freshener to cover the smell of the burning plastic."

Hawk shook his head. "Jill, you're getting the hang of cop humor."

A tall, slender man wearing a t-shirt and cut-off shorts appeared behind the screen. "Um, Ranger Washington, what can I do for you?"

"My colleagues and I are investigating the disappearance of the surveyors. May we come in?"

The man looked over his shoulder. "Um, we don't know anything about the surveyors."

"One of you might've noticed something the day they disappeared without even realizing it."

Jill stepped next to Hawk. "There may have been something incidental that happened, a strange vehicle passing by, or something that just seemed out of place or wrong. We'd really appreciate your help."

Jill's unassuming appeal for assistance disarmed the man. He glanced at the badge on her belt and gun. "Are you undercover cops?"

"We're National Park Service investigators from Texas. We've been asked to assist with the investigation into the missing surveyors. May we come in and talk to all of your team?"

Reluctantly, the man pushed the screen door open and stood back so we could pass.

Three women and a man sat around a scarred wooden table on rickety chairs, trying hard to look nonchalant in the marijuana smoke haze. Two of the women wore tank tops, and as Hawk had predicted, tufts of hair were visible in their armpits. I tried hard to stifle my smile over their hippie appearance and effort to appear innocent about the marijuana.

The third woman, chunkier than the others and maybe twenty years older, stood and offered us chairs. "Would you like a cup of tea brewed from local herbs?"

Jill smiled but shook her head. "No thanks."

"I'll take a cup," Hawk said, surprising me. He sat in the chair at the head of the table, facing the others and the entry door. "What blend are you brewing today, Bella?"

Bella, wearing a summery dress, took a pot off the stove. "We picked lemon balm, lemongrass, borage, and chamomile." She poured steaming water into a teapot, then added herbs to a stainless-steel tea ball and put it into the teapot.

Jill looked around the kitchen, which was surprisingly neat and clean. A pot boiled on the stove, and next to it, a cutting board was piled with cubed carrots, turnips, onions, and okra. The cupboards were painted white, and the countertops were linoleum curled in the corners. There wasn't a dirty dish in sight. "You don't have electricity. I see kerosene lamps, like the ones we kept on the ranch in case the power went out."

Bella set the teapot on the table and went to the cupboard. She took out two mugs, then looked at Jill and me. "Are you sure you won't have some tea? I promise I'm not trying to poison you."

Hawk nodded. "Bella's teas are tasty and healthy, and the lemon balm will cure ailments from anxiety to menstrual cramps."

"Sure, I'll have a cup," I said, taking a chair facing the living room. "I don't suppose there's anything in your tea to cure my partner's hot flashes."

Jill gave me the evil eye, then nodded to Bella. "I'll have a cup, too."

I heard the floor creaking above us and looked at the man who'd opened the door. "You have more of your team upstairs?"

Standing next to the door with his arms crossed, he nodded. "Kai's our night owl. He's just getting up."

The woman set the mugs on the table. "I apologize for Ned. I'm Isabella, but everyone calls me Bella. Jen's sitting next to me. Tina is at the end, and Bruce is sitting next to her."

"I'm Doug Fletcher, and this is Jill, my partner. You already know Ranger Washington."

Bella set the teapot on the table and sat down. "You're investigating the disappearance of a survey crew?"

Jill fingered her empty mug. "They disappeared Monday, and neither surveyor nor their truck has been seen since then. We hoped one of you may have seen something unusual or a strange vehicle passing while you were protesting."

Bella poured a bit of tea into a mug, releasing a lovely lemony aroma. She tasted it, then poured some for us. "I'm the house mom, so I'm not out on the drill sites. Tina, you were out all Monday. Did you see anything odd?"

Tina's dark hair and skin appeared to reflect her Mexican heritage. Her clothes weren't tattered, and her hair looked like it had been cut professionally, unlike the other women who wore their hair in braids, ponytails, or cornrows. She fidgeted nervously like a child called on in class that didn't know the answer to the posed question. "I, um, don't remember anything strange. Most days are pretty much the same."

"Did you notice any unusual vehicles?" Jill asked, sniffing her tea but waiting for it to cool before sipping.

Tina shook her head. "There are different cars and minivans every day, and tourists going east and west, and a few local people in pickups and old cars. I don't remember anything out of the ordinary."

"Do you remember the surveyors' truck passing?"

"I've seen it, but I don't remember if they passed us on Monday."

I nodded toward the ceiling. "I'd like to talk to your upstairs friend."

An uneasy look passed among the people around the table before Bella responded, "Kai's been at the house all the time. He won't know anything."

Jill sipped her tea. "Is there some reason you don't want us to speak with Kai?"

Bella's look was unreadable. "He's not a morning person."

"I hear him moving around," Jill replied.

Bella hesitated. I expected her to go upstairs or yell for Kai, and instead, she grabbed the broom from the corner. I somehow expected her to sweep and stall but was surprised when she used the broom handle to thump the kitchen ceiling three times. The response came as three thumps from above. "He'll be right down."

The staircase creaked as Kai walked down. I saw bare feet and dark workout pants first. Then a thick bare chest and biceps as large as my thighs. Kai's facial features were Oriental, and his short-cropped hair topped a head that sloped out to his shoulders, leaving no discernable neck. His look of contempt didn't soften when he saw Jill and me at the table.

His eyes drifted to Hawk, and his frown disappeared. "Ah, my Native brother, Ranger Washington. What brings you to our mosquito-infested haven?"

I watched Jill sizing up Kai, from narrow hips to broad, hairless chest, massive arms and neck reminiscent of a football player or weightlifter. She glanced at me, but her expression was unreadable.

Bella poured another mug of tea and set it at the empty spot. The wooden chair groaned under Kai's weight. "Kai, the ranger asked if we knew anything about the missing surveyors."

In Kai's huge hand, the ceramic mug looked like a cup from a child's tea set. He wrapped his fingers around it, making me wonder if his sausage-sized fingers fit inside the handle. "I don't go to the drilling sites with the others, so no, I didn't even know there were missing surveyors," he said.

Bella looked at me. "Kai's our security person."

The pieces fell into place. Kai was the night owl and security person. "Has there been any trouble around the house?"

Kai drank tea, then shook his head. "A couple pickups came down the driveway the first week we were here, and I talked with them. None of them have been back."

Jill leaned on the table. "Obviously, you can take care of yourself, but a lot of the locals have guns in their pickups. You're muscular but not bulletproof."

Kai nodded toward the front door. "I've got a Remington tactical shotgun with buckshot loads. Between seeing me and the shotgun, people tend to just back out of the driveway and not return."

Hawk smiled. "I think you should accompany the women when they go grocery shopping."

Kai nodded. "I have since the 'incident.'"

"You haven't seen the surveyors' truck," Jill said, making a statement rather than a question.

"Like I said, I'm not out on the highway with the others."

"That's not the same as no."

I think if either Hawk or I made that comment, it would've been received poorly. Coming from Jill, it was just a comment.

"No. The only time I would've seen them is if they'd driven down the driveway at night, and they haven't been here."

Bella shook her head. "They were here one morning when Kai was asleep. A man and woman drove a blue pickup into the driveway. They asked if we were the property owners, and when I said no, they left."

"They haven't done any surveys in this area?" I asked.

"Not that we know about."

Jill swirled her teacup and drank the last swallow. "And if they had come in here to survey, what would you have done?"

Bella flattened her hands on the table. "We're non-violent, so certainly would've expressed our displeasure with the oil drilling operations and explained our position, but we wouldn't harm them."

I looked at Kai. "You agree?"

"I'm a third-level karate blackbelt, and I've been trained in self-discipline and respect. The shotgun and I are here for self-defense. If I assault someone or fire the gun, it'll be in response to provocation."

Hawk stood. "Thanks for the tea."

The protesters stood, except for Kai. Jill got up and looked at him. "You don't seem to fit in with this bunch."

He shrugged and got up, looking even more menacing when I realized he was five or six inches taller than me. "Who pays your salary?" I asked.

Bella was ready to protest, but I put up my hand.

"Them," he replied, nodding toward Bella.

I looked at the rest of the group. Their tattered clothes and hippie vibe didn't fit with Kai. "I doubt that."

"Believe what you want," he replied, turning away and going back up the stairs.

The young protesters stayed inside. I hung back with Bella while Jill and Hawk walked to the car. "You're lucky to have Kai here. I don't think this is a very hospitable place for your crowd."

Bella looked into the swamp. "Yeah, mosquitoes, alligators, feral pigs, and more."

I faced her. "I was talking about the people."

Bella crossed her arms. "They leave us alone."

"I disagree. There was the grocery store incident and the night visitors Kai chased off." I paused. "I assume you have a cellphone."

She looked into my eyes and nodded. "It's turned off most of the time. I charge it when we drive into town."

"The response time for a 911 call might be uncomfortably long."

She looked away into the swamp. "We know that it's part of the risk in protecting the environment."

"You understand that the drilling is legal, and it's not going to stop."

"Maybe not now, but more people are listening all the time. If we don't raise the issue, who will?" She paused. "Are you trying to scare us away?"

"Not at all. I'm sworn to uphold the constitution and the laws of the land. I've got no problem with you as long as you're obeying the law."

I turned to leave but felt Bella's hand on my arm. "Would you respond if I called 911?"

"It's not my jurisdiction."

"That's not what I'm asking. If you heard the call, would you come to our aid?"

"Yes, of course."

"I'm not convinced every law enforcement person down here feels the same way."

"I think Hawk does."

Bella nodded. "He gave me his cellphone number."

I took out a business card and handed it to her. "Jill and I will only be here through the investigation, but I guarantee we'll come to your aid if you call us."

"Jill's more than your partner."

"Yes, we're married."

Bella smiled. "You're happily married, and you respect each other. That's a rare combination."

"How long have you been divorced?"

"I've been divorced longer than I was married." Bella nodded toward the idling pickup. "Your partners are waiting for you."

I got in the back seat and buckled my seat belt. "I'm glad they've got Kai for security. This would be a scary place without him."

Hawk turned the truck around in the yard. "I'm not sure it's a lot less scary with him."

Jill looked over her shoulder. "You had a long discussion. Did you learn anything?"

"Bella is convinced no one would quickly respond if she dialed 911."

Jill nodded. "This place is remote."

Hawk glanced at Jill. "Bella and I have had this discussion, and she's also convinced the local cops wouldn't rush to their aid."

"Well, would they?" Jill asked.

"They're professionals, Jill, just like anywhere else. Like you said, this is a remote place, and the chances of a county deputy or trooper being within half an hour of here is unlikely. I'm sure Bella would think they're ignoring her call because they're prejudiced against them."

"I suppose the protesters are a bunch of city kids used to multiple police cars responding in minutes to an emergency call. Growing up on a ranch, I learned very early on that the deputies were our friends, but they probably won't be close if we dialed 911."

Hawk pulled out of the driveway onto the highway. "I suppose you grew up with a shotgun behind the kitchen door."

"A shotgun behind the door and a pistol on my hip."

"You carried a pistol around?"

"From the time I knew how to shoot until the Park Service hired me."

"I knew there was something I liked about you. I want to marry a woman who knows how to shoot." Hawk glanced in the rearview mirror at me, then looked at Jill. "Give me a call if you ever decide to kick Doug to the curb."

Jill laughed and shook her head. "I'm old enough to be your mother."

"You wouldn't consider dating a younger man?"

"I've already got one of those." Jill looked over her shoulder, "And the experiment is ongoing."

Hawk looked surprised. "You're older than Doug?"

"Be careful, Hawk. She's a cougar."

"Let's get serious," Jill said. "I don't like the look of Kai, and something seems off about him."

"He's a bodyguard," I said. "He may not share their cause, but he's there to protect them."

"His eyes were…"

Hawk nodded. "He's professionally detached, and I think all good security people stay detached from their clients."

Jill shook her head. "You're not listening. I think he's capable of killing someone."

"I agree," I said from the back. "But Kai didn't shoot the surveyors. A gun isn't his weapon of choice. His body is."

Jill considered my arguments, then moved on. "Hawk, you had some additional spots you would've looked at if we hadn't dragged you away this morning. Let's check them out."

"Actually, my breakfast has worn off, and whatever the hippies were cooking smelled pretty good."

"I didn't know Yankees ate possum."

"Possum?" I asked.

"You didn't see the skins nailed to the outhouse?"

"I thought the protesters were probably vegan," I replied.

"Not all of them and not today. I've got water, sandwiches, and chips in the cooler."

Jill drew a deep breath. "I'm sorry, but I don't think I'm up for Spam today."

Hawk perked up. "I sensed your…aversion to the Spam, so I went to the store and bought real lunch meat."

I lifted the cooler and set it on my lap. "Are we going to eat on the fly, or are you going to stop somewhere and picnic?"

"I think there's a regulation about eating and driving. In about a mile, there's a place we can pull over."

Jill glanced over her shoulder. "What do you consider *real* lunch meat, Hawk?"

"You've got your choice of bologna or olive and pimento loaf."

Jill coughed, usually a sign that something I was about to choose from a menu was making her gag.

Hawk started laughing and wiped his eyes. "Jill, you are so predictable. You've got your choice of ham or turkey on whole-wheat bread. There are little packets of mayo and mustard in the bottom of the cooler."

Hawk's tears made Jill laugh, too. "I may need to eat a package of mustard. Just the thought of an olive and pimento loaf sandwich made me throw up in my mouth."

Sitting side-by-side on the tailgate, we ate sandwiches and speculated on the group of people gathered at what Hawk called the commune. "I haven't seen the upstairs," Hawk said, "But there can't be more than three bedrooms. I've seen nine people at the house or protesting. I wonder if this is like a free-love commune or if they've got bunk beds in each room?"

Jill shuddered. "I helped my mom clean out the rough bunkhouse after the roundup and sale, and the level of hygiene and cleanliness that I'm accustomed to is not easy to maintain with an outhouse and an outdoor solar shower."

I crumpled my potato chip bag and put it into the cooler. "I didn't see any clotheslines in the back. They must take their dirty clothes to a laundromat."

Hawk nodded. "Clothes don't dry well in this humidity, so I'm sure they're using the laundromat in Sweetwater."

Jill ate the last bite of her turkey sandwich and wiped the breadcrumbs off her lap. "Before we rudely interrupted your day, Hawk, where were you going to search for the surveyors?"

"There are only a few places where you can cross the canals. I was going to check the two ahead of us, toward Sweetwater. I've looked at every other place with highway access."

"Then what?" I asked.

"Phew! I suppose I'd probably talk to the airboat operators and fishing guides to see if they've spotted anything. After that, I'm out of ideas."

"What do you think about Butch Conley?" Jill asked. "You said you didn't like the idea of knocking on his door, not knowing if he had a shotgun aimed from the other side."

"Yeah, I was kind of dramatic. Butch is an idiot hothead. He's a bigot, so he doesn't like Hal Rude or me, but I don't know that he'd actually shoot anyone who knocked on his door."

I drank the last of my water and put the bottle in the cooler. "But we're Yankee cops, and we won't be his favorite people either."

Hawk smiled. "Maybe you could try speaking with a southern accent."

Jill choked on her last swallow of water. "Do I look like a debutante?"

Hawk put his sandwich and potato chip bags into the cooler and closed it. "Put on your boots. We're going walking."

* * *

The two areas Hawk had in mind were swampy with some high ground where he parked, but we waded through shallow water among the cypress stands for hours. The first tract of land looked like no one had been in it for months. The grass was undisturbed, and no signs the surveyors, or anyone else, had been there recently.

191

The second area was closer to our cabin. Across the canal was a rough road of packed shells and gravel. We drove into an open glade hidden by cypress trees, and tire tracks were evident in the tufts of grass on the road.

"Someone's been back here," Jill observed.

"This is more accessible to people coming through from the west," Hawk said. "I think it's a party place for local teens because I always find trash and tire tracks back here."

Hawk parked on the road at the edge of an open grassy area. Orange plastic ribbon was tied to a wooden stake on the left side of the road. I recognized the cryptic marking on the stick as a surveyors' description of a corner. "Looks like the survey crew has been here."

Jill smeared insect repellent on her arms and legs, then handed the bottle to me. "I see at least two sets of tire prints ahead of us."

Squatting down, Hawk studied a muddy spot in the single-lane road. "I see three or four different tracks."

"We're blocking the egress," I said as I applied insect repellent.

"Yup. If there's anyone back here, they'll have to stop here so we can chat."

I offered the insect repellent to Hawk, who declined. "The road splits twice, each branch going to open areas the drilling companies would like to test for oil and gas deposits."

We'd walked maybe a hundred yards when I noticed another strip of orange plastic gently waving from a tree branch. "The surveyors had to wade far into the swamp to hang that survey marker."

Hawk nodded. "They slog through a lot of nasty areas to do their jobs. Being a surveyor here is challenging, lonely work. The two-person crews spend a lot of time together in remote places. From what I understand, they develop a sense of what has to happen. One person operates the laser transit, and the helper moves a rod with a reflector on it. They use hand signals to define corners and distances. Someone told me the partners become attuned to each other and anticipate the other person's needs and moves, like a surgeon and a surgical nurse."

"The Everglades City surveyors were a male/female team," Jill observed. "I wonder if anything was going on between them?"

Hawk walked as he thought. "I didn't get a sense of that from talking with Paul, the owner's son."

"He works alone in the office and might not be the best person to sense the vibe between Terri and his dad."

"I don't know. It seems like a stretch to think they had something going. So, you're thinking they were fooling around, and someone caught onto it and killed them?"

"Doug always says that love, money, and drugs are the most likely murder motives." Jill looked at me. "Right?"

"We always consider the spouses or significant others first, then work down the list from there. It's really rare for someone to be killed by a stranger unless they get shot during a holdup or a drug buy that's gone bad."

"I talked to Mike Lawler's wife on Tuesday after she reported him missing. She was a wreck, and Terri Smith's ex-husband was dazed." Hawk paused, reflecting on the conversations. "His new wife was angry about being stuck with Terri's kids rather than being mad at Terri, and I'm sure she isn't the killer."

"You ruled them out as the murderers immediately," Jill said.

"Yeah. I feel confident they're not the killers. We can talk with a few of the airboat and fishing charters while we're driving to Everglades City."

Jill stopped abruptly and stuck out her hand. I'd seen her make that gesture when she'd seen a rattlesnake in Arizona. I looked to the ground and reached for my pistol. I saw nothing, but adrenaline coursed through my system. "What?" I whispered.

She pointed ahead. "I see a car's taillight."

Hawk nodded and walked ahead slowly. "We've been following fresh tire tracks."

The underbrush had obscured the older, gray, double-cab pickup that became visible as we followed the curving trail. The windows were rolled down, one back door was open, and music played softly. We stopped twenty yards away from the truck and surveyed the area.

Jill walked to the edge of the road, looking beyond the front of the truck. "I don't see anyone picnicking," she whispered.

Hawk gave me a knowing look. "I think someone's knocking boots in the back seat."

Jill turned and glared at him. "What makes you say that?"

Raising his eyebrows suggestively, Hawk smiled. "People come here to be out of sight."

We were walking ahead slowly when I heard a slap. A woman exclaimed, "Damned mosquitoes." Next came a whiff of cigarette smoke, followed by a giggle.

Jill froze and looked at us. "Let's leave them alone."

I rubbed my nose to hide my smile. "We have to ask if they saw the surveyors."

"No, we really don't," Jill said in an outdoor voice, causing a flurry of activity in the back of the truck.

A cigarette flicked out of the window. Heads bobbed in the rear window and muffled voices conveyed a sense of urgency. A man sat up, then slid out of the open door as he pulled on his boots.

"What can I do for y'all?"

Hawk was nonchalant. "We're searching for missing surveyors. I don't suppose you've seen them or their blue pickup?"

"Um, no. I haven't seen anyone at all."

"How about your friend? Has she seen anyone?"

Mussed blonde hair popped into view. The woman squirmed, apparently putting on some piece of clothing. Slipping barefoot from the other side of the truck, all that was visible were her lower legs, bare feet, and blonde head. She stepped around the door and faced us. "I haven't seen anyone, either." She glanced at Jill and me, but her eyes locked on Hawk, making her blush.

"Hi, Charlene. They disappeared Monday. Were you guys out here then?"

The woman's eyes narrowed. "We were not out here Monday or any other day. I'm not in the habit..." She realized what she was about to say and stopped. "No."

Her male partner wore a silly grin rather than a look of shame. "No, sir. This is the first time we've been here this week."

Charlene looked over the pickup bed at the younger man. "Shut up, Tommy."

He shrugged. "No, we haven't been here since lunchtime last Friday."

"Dammit, Tommy, stop talking."

Hawk raised his hands. "I don't really care if you're here every day, Charlene. I only wanted to know about the surveyors."

"I don't know a thing about them. Okay?"

"Have a nice day," Hawk said as he turned away and gestured for us to follow. "That's Charlene, the bank loan officer's wife, and Tommy is their neighbor."

"Are you going to mention this to anyone?" Jill asked.

"I won't, but I'm sure it'll come to light."

Jill shook her head. "I suppose this will lead to a divorce."

"I don't think so. Charlene's husband has been known to negotiate some loans in St. Pete." Hawk paused. "He and Charlene probably have an understanding. She doesn't out him, and she finds romance where she can."

"Out him?" Jill asked.

"It's rumored that he prefers men to women, but that wouldn't go over well in a small-town bank. So he married Charlene, and they show up together at community functions. A plumber I know said they have separate bedrooms in their big house."

"But sex with your neighbor?"

Hawk turned his head toward Jill. "They're adults."

Jill drew a deep breath and blew it out. "I wonder if anything like this happens in South Dakota?"

I laughed. "You are so naïve, dear. Things like this happen everywhere. Don't you remember our discussion with Michele, the forensic genealogist? She said about ten percent of the family trees she creates have a child whose male parent isn't the genetic father."

"I thought she meant over dozens of generations."

"She meant every generation, over hundreds of years."

Hawk smiled. "That kind of history ensures genetic diversity."

Jill looked back when we heard the argument behind us. "I think that attempt at genetic diversity may have ended poorly."

Hawk shrugged. "I suspect Charlene will find pollen from a different flower."

Jill looked at me. "Men are pigs."

Hawk stopped and stared at Jill. "You're mistaken about the aggressor in this case. Charlene is known as the local amusement park."

"Amusement park?" Jill asked.

Hawk smirked, ready to deliver the punchline. "Everyone's gone for a ride."

Jill glared at me. "My comment stands, men are pigs, and they're taking advantage of a woman who's got obvious emotional problems...then they're compounding the insult by calling her an amusement park."

"Hey! I've never cheated on you!"

"We've only been married a little over a year, and maybe you haven't met the Texas version of Charlene yet."

I grabbed her hand and squeezed it. "Not all men are pigs, and not all women are like Charlene. I take my marriage vows seriously."

I felt her squeeze my fingers. "I was just venting."

The sound of an engine starting behind us stirred Hawk to pick up the pace. "We have to move the truck, so Charlene can get back to her job before her lunch break is over."

# Chapter 11

We visited two vendors offering airboat rides. Half the boats were out, so we didn't get to speak to every captain, but those we interviewed had seen the surveyors' truck at some point but didn't recall anything unusual about Monday. As expected, none of them had seen the surveyors or their vehicle since Monday.

A gray-haired captain with the unlikely moniker, Sonny, sighed when we asked him about the surveyors. Sonny's face, neck, and arms were deeply tanned, and his neck seemed like the Grand Canyon with all its tributaries. He spat a stream of tobacco juice off the dock, then said, "I don't know about them specifically, but in general, I think they're crazy fools. They're traipsing around in the swamp among the cottonmouths, gators, and dozens of other critters that want to either bite you, eat you, or suck your blood."

I could tell Jill liked Sonny, probably because he bore a slight resemblance to her Uncle Chet. "How long have you been doing this?"

Sonny spat another stream of tobacco juice, narrowly missing an egret who was fishing just below us. "Well, I've driven an airboat all my adult life, but it's just been the last dozen years I've been taking out tourists."

"What did you do before?"

Sonny laughed with a rasp that turned into a coughing fit. "Nothin' I'd admit to a game warden. Blink, the owner, asked me to fill in for a day, and I'll be damned if one day's tips weren't more than I was making in a month of poaching gators and snaring..." He paused and looked at Hawk's uniform, then our badges. "Well, doing other stuff."

Jill smiled. "We're not going to arrest you. But we'd like to hear what you think might've happened to the surveyors. Two are missing, along with their truck."

Pushing the tobacco under his lip with his tongue, he thought. "Well, they're local folks, so I imagine they know better than to drive into one of the canals. I s'pose they got mired deep off one of the trails and..."

"And what?"

"It's not like the old days. You'd get stuck somewhere, and it'd take a whole day to walk out and hitch a ride home to get a tractor or mules. Now, everyone has a damned cell phone jammed in their ear. They can't be away from their friends for five minutes without texting or calling them."

201

Sonny looked at Jill. "I don't s'pose they called anyone for help."

"No."

Sonny spat another stream of tobacco juice. "They're likely dead and in the swamp."

"I think so too, but I can't find their truck."

Sonny pushed his bulbous nose around with the palm of his hand, then pulled a red bandana out of his back pocket and wiped his upper lip. "There are lots of ways of making a pickup disappear."

I could tell Jill was having a good time buttering up Sonny. "Really? Like what?"

Sonny leaned close like he was about to whisper a secret. "Most aren't legal."

"There's more than one way to get rid of a truck?"

"The easiest is to park it in an old barn and sell off all the pieces. Hell, a truck's worth more one-piece at a time than it is to buy it whole." Sonny twitched his nose like it itched. "Or people swap out the license plates from their broken-down truck. It's not like the highway cops are going to check the identification number if the plates are for the right make and year."

"Wow, I've led a sheltered life. I'd never think of those things."

Sonny puffed up. "My money would be on parting it out. It's more work, but hell, there's lots of folks around here with time on their hands. They'll sell off everything but the frame, and then they sell that for scrap metal. I've seen that surveyors' truck, and it's darned close to new. Those parts would be worth a lot."

"I suppose we should be talking to junkyards."

Sonny smiled and shook his head. "Pull out your computer and see who's selling parts there. Hell, a set of rims with good truck tires might sell for a thousand bucks, and that alone is a lot of money for someone trying to scratch a living out of the ground around here."

"No one's going to kill two surveyors for the parts off their truck."

Sonny rolled the tobacco wad around his mouth. "No good Christian folk would, but there are some shady characters in this world. Your partners could probably tell you stories that'd curl the hair on your pretty head."

Jill smiled and glanced at me. "Oh, they've tried, but I just ignore them."

Sonny's smile disappeared. "You're not that crazy lady ranger who swam out and pulled Cuban kids out of the van, are you?"

"That must've been some other crazy woman."

Sonny stared into Jill's eyes. "Ma'am, you don't seem crazy, but it seems like you're awfully good-hearted to be a cop. I think it was you who saved those kids." He looked at me. "It was her, right?"

I nodded.

Sonny reached out his hand and shook Jill's. "I'm not much of a one for supporting illegal immigrants, but good on you for saving those kids. That took some balls."

Jill smiled at Sonny's political incorrectness. "I guess I'll have to grow a pair of them."

Sonny waved off her comment. "Not many people put themselves out there like that. You're special."

"Thank you."

"If you ever want to take an airboat ride, come see me."

"Maybe after we find the surveyors and their truck."

"You're wasting your time. They're long gone."

"Do you know more than you're saying?"

"Naw. I've just lived in the swamp for a long time. When people and things aren't seen for a few days, they're generally gone for good."

I walked to the truck, digesting Sonny's words. "Who else would want them dead?"

"Sex, money, and drugs," Jill repeated. "Were they into drugs? Did they stumble onto someone's drug operation?"

Hawk stopped at the truck's bumper. "There's a smuggling trade down here, with people bringing drugs into the Thousand Islands area from the Caribbean. Small boats pick up the shipments and move them ashore, and I don't see how legitimate surveyors would get tangled up in that."

"Was the business in trouble?" Jill asked. "Maybe Mike turned to drug smuggling to save it."

I mulled that thought. "It looked like Paul Lawler was struggling to keep up with all the survey documents they were generating. If anything, it looked like they could've hired another person in the office to help out."

"Maybe Terri dumped a boyfriend," Jill suggested. "He might've been angry."

Hawk wrinkled his nose. "She and Mike worked long hours, and then she had two kids under her care. I don't know when she'd have had time for a relationship. I'm more inclined to think they stumbled onto a meth operation."

"There wasn't any sign of meth cooking where we found the blood," I said. "If the surveyors had stumbled on that somewhere else, why would they take them to that remote location to kill them?"

We got in the truck and waited for the air conditioning to kick in. Hawk looked over his shoulder at me. "I'm out of ideas."

"Drop us at the cabin, and we'll kick it around for the night. Maybe I'll have some other avenue to pursue in the morning."

Pulling onto the highway, Hawk sighed. "Tomorrow is Saturday. I've got a wedding to attend in the evening, so I'll only be able to spend a couple hours with you."

Jill shook her head. "Take the weekend off, Hawk. We sometimes lose track of people's personal time when we're away from home on an investigation. If we come up with some thoughts, we can pursue them, and we'll jump back into it with you on Monday."

"Are you sure? We're past the 48-hour mark, and the case is getting colder."

Jill looked over her shoulder, hinting that I should weigh in on the conversation. "We're out of ideas. Let's think about the case over the weekend. We'll meet you Monday morning for breakfast, and we'll brainstorm then."

Hawk stopped in front of the campground office and slipped the pickup into park. "I hate to bail on you guys."

Waving off his concern, Jill grabbed the door handle. "It'll be good to take a break and look at this with fresh eyes after the weekend. Enjoy the wedding."

Jill was deep in thought as we walked to the cabin. "I'll call the travel office and have them rebook our return flights."

"Mrs. Fletcher, you've become a real cop."

Jill stopped and stared at me. "What led you to that conclusion?"

"Park Superintendent Rickowski would've been concerned about the rebooking cost and the lack of any active leads to pursue. That previous version of you still had an administrator mindset, and the new you, Inspector Fletcher, is ready to let the Park Service pay for rebooking flights because she feels like she's on a scent."

Chuckling, Jill started walking. "It's your fault. You've convinced me there's never a dead end."

"The investigation is more important than the budget," I said.

Jill stopped at the cabin's steps. "Let's go to Joanie's for supper. I'll call Matt on the way there and tell him we're staying a few more days."

I nodded toward the cabin. "Do you want to change first?"

"Crap! All my new clothes are still in Hawk's truck." Jill pulled out her new phone as we walked back toward the campground office. "He's not picking up."

When I started laughing, Jill disconnected the call. "What?"

"Look who's walking this way, carrying shopping bags."

Hawk held out the shopping bags to Jill. "I thought you might want these."

Smiling, Jill accepted the bags. "I was just calling you."

"I was reaching for a bottle of water in the cooler when I saw your shopping bags in the back seat. I thought you'd want the fresh clothes before Monday."

Jill followed Hawk back to the campground parking lot, thanking him profusely. "We're going to Joanie's for supper. Would you like to join us?"

"I appreciate the offer but, I've got other plans."

Jill smiled. "You've got a date."

"A friend invited me over for supper."

Jill was about to grill Hawk for details, but I interrupted. "Have fun. We'll see you Monday morning." I clicked the key fob and opened the rental car's trunk. "Throw your bags in the trunk. We're going to eat."

Deep in thought, Jill stared out the window as I drove. "I'm pleased Hawk has a girlfriend. He's a nice guy."

"We've probably messed up his personal life this week, but that's how investigations go."

"I think Hawk's found this interesting. He'll be back to his usual routine when we're gone." Jill paused. "We've been a break in his monotonous life. He's probably filling his friend in on all the excitement we've provided."

Joanie's parking lot was packed, and people lined up outside the door. I parked, and we walked to the back of the line. Jill grabbed my arm and leaned close to my ear. "Don't you dare cut ahead in the line and use your badge to get preferred seating."

"We might get an emergency call."

Jill pulled out her phone and punched in a number. "I need to call Matt anyway, so we can wait in line just like the other people."

"Whatever."

Jill waited while the phone rang. "Mandy, how are you?"

I leaned close and whispered, "I thought you were calling Matt, not his wife."

Jill pushed me away. "We're in a restaurant line waiting to be seated. What's new in Texas?"

I took out my phone and punched in a South Dakota number from memory. "Chet, how are you and Mom?"

Chet, my mother's fiancé, was a man of few words. He greeted me and quickly handed the phone to my mother, Ronnie. "Doug, I'm surprised that you called. I usually have to call Jill to get any information. Has she dried out from her swim in the pond?"

"She's still got a bathroom full of damp clothes. But she's dry and is coping. We heard that most of the kids she helped are okay."

"Most are okay, but not all?"

"They're waiting to see if the little boy, who was in the van the longest, has suffered any permanent problems."

"What kind of problems?"

I made sure Jill had engaged in Mandy's discussion, then I turned away. "He might have brain damage from lack of oxygen."

Mom sighed. "That'll be hard on Jill."

"We may hear more about him next week. Jill's being distracted by other things for now."

"Have you found the missing people yet?"

"Not yet, but we're moving ahead."

"Please take care of her, Doug."

"I always take care of her."

There was a long pause followed by the sound of a door closing. "You do NOT always take care of her. You put her in situations where her body and soul are at risk."

"She's with me."

"Douglas, that's not terribly reassuring. You do reckless things."

I moved ahead with the line and pulled Jill's elbow. "Have a nice evening, Mom."

"You're being evasive."

"We're in the restaurant now. I have to hang up."

"You're trying to get rid of me."

"Bye, Mom."

I ended the call and looked at Jill, who was smiling and still talking to Mandy, who was able to put a smile on anyone's face— no better therapy than a conversation with Mandy.

We reached the steps at Joanie's Crab Shack, and I tapped Jill on the shoulder. "We're nearly inside the restaurant. Tell Mandy to say hi to Matt."

Jill ended the call and turned to me. "Who did you call?"

"I talked to Mom. She scolded me for not taking better care of you."

"What does she expect you to do?"

"Not drag you into dangerous situations that risk your life and mess with your mind."

"I love Ronnie. She blames you for the questionable things I do. I couldn't ask for a better mother-in-law."

I was shaking my head when we got to the counter. "It looks like tonight's special is stuffed crab."

"What's it stuffed with?"

"How should I know?"

A middle-aged woman behind us overheard our conversation and leaned close. "It's bread stuffing with crab meat, celery, and spices like a crab cake stuffed in a crab shell. It's to die for, and so popular they sometimes run out before everyone gets through the line."

"It's got celery, so there's a vegetable," I said, smiling.

A waitress who'd served us before grabbed two menus and motioned for us to follow. She took us to a booth near the kitchen and handed us the menus, then leaned close. "You can look at the menu, but I recommend the stuffed crab. Order now, and I'll make sure your order gets filled before the kitchen runs out."

Handing her the menu, I looked at Jill. "I'm having the special."

Jill nodded. "That and unsweet tea."

The waitress was gone before I could order a beer. I reasoned there was plenty of beer but not so many stuffed crabs. Conversation and laughter filled the noisy room. "Mandy worked her magic?"

"Her world is a happy, fun place, and somehow she takes me along for the ride."

I reached out and took Jill's hand. "She's a gift."

"I told Matt what's going on and that we were rebooking our return flights."

"I assume he okayed that."

The smile melted from Jill's face, and she pulled her hand back. "Matt told me that Hawk's video is on Reuters news service and the networks."

"I'm sure they're pleased to share happy news given all the other things that are going on."

Jill drew a deep breath and blew it out. "Mandy said the same thing, but it's just that..."

Our waitress set down Jill's tea and a bottle of beer before Jill completed her thought. "There's plenty of crab, so I'll grab two cups of chowder to tide you over until the crabs are out of the oven."

Jill squeezed lemon into her tea and stirred it. "What are we going to do this weekend?"

"What would you like to do?"

"I'd like to sleep until noon, soak in the bath, take an airboat ride, and hike one of the trails near the visitor center. What would you like to do?"

"I'll skip the soak in the bathtub, but the rest sounds good to me."

Two cups of seafood chowder arrived with packages of crackers and reminded me of the tomato-based cioppino we'd had on the opposite side of Florida.

Jill stirred the chowder and examined the bits of meat swirling in the broth. "There's okra in this."

"So?"

"It's not a judgment, just a comment." She blew on a spoonful of chowder, then sipped it. Her eyes lit up. "This is really good."

I ate a spoonful and nodded my agreement. "I just don't want to think about the little cubes of meat."

Jill wrinkled her nose. "It's chicken."

I laughed. "It tastes just like chicken."

Jill raised her hand before I could add to the comment. "Just leave it at that, okay?"

The crabs arrived before we finished the chowder. The top of each crab had been removed, and brown stuffing, dotted with chunks of white crab meat and green celery, overflowed the shell. "You two good for now, or do you need drink refills?"

I shook my head, barely having touched my beer.

Jill held up her glass. "Unsweet tea, please." She tentatively lifted a piece of stuffing from the crab and blew on it gently before sliding it into her mouth. She started huffing and grabbed my beer, drinking a quarter of it in one swallow. "HOT!"

I laughed and spread pieces of stuffing around my plate to cool. The waitress returned with Jill's glass of tea. Seeing my cooling plan, she nodded. "I should've warned you. They're very hot."

As the waitress walked away, Jill leaned close. "Hot hardly describes the temperature."

I ate one of the cooled pieces and savored the wonderful flavor. "I hope you can taste this after burning your tongue. It's really good."

Jill shared tidbits of her conversation with Mandy, ranging from her golf group to Matt's struggles with the new law enforcement ranger. "Mandy says he's a bit uptight, and he's not content to warn people and lecture about littering. He's lecturing and getting in people's faces.

"Yeah, I've known a few cops like that. It's usually the ones who are just past their probationary period and feel like they need to exercise power. I'll talk with him when we get back."

"Mandy said the Port Aransas library re-opened. It's taken them three years since Hurricane Harvey to repair, rebuild, and restock it."

"Yeah, it's painful to see all the boarded-up businesses, condos, and houses around town."

Jill finished her crab and stuffed her napkin in the empty shell. "That was really good. I'm going to visit the ladies' room. Do *not* order key lime pie for me." She stood then edged past tables to the restrooms on the opposite side of the dining room.

I was reading the dessert options on the blackboard when I saw Jill stop abruptly halfway across the room. She reached down and grabbed a guy's wrist. "You grab my ass again, and you'll lose that hand!"

I stood, but Jill was on the move again before I took a step. A young guy rubbed his wrist while his three buddies threw insults about his lack of manhood. His face was getting red, and I assumed he wouldn't take the ribbing without defending himself.

"I ain't never seen a lady cop before," said one of the buddies. "Looks like she could take you, though."

"Naw, she's a skinny thing. I could probably make her cry just by standing up and giving her my *look*."

As the banter continued, the volume went up, and it became clear the well-liquored boys planned another go-around with Jill when she passed. I stood to meet Jill halfway across the floor until a burly guy with his back to the smart-mouthed guys angrily threw his napkin on his plate.

He was barrel-chested and had muscular arms. The banter stopped when the young men saw him staring down at them. He put his ham-sized hand on the younger man's shoulder, then apparently squeezed as he leaned close. I couldn't hear what he said, but the young men got very quiet. When he stood up, the young men dug cash out of their wallets and threw it on the table, then made a beeline for the door.

When Jill came out of the ladies' room, they were gone, but the big man was still standing. Jill threaded her way through the tables, stopping at the big guy, who stretched out his hand and shook hers. He leaned close, said something that made her smile, then he picked up the money from the young men's table and delivered it to the cash register.

Jill sat down, then looked back at the man having an earnest discussion with the hostess. "That was odd."

"What did he say to you?"

"He apologized for the 'boys' and asked if I was the park ranger he'd seen on the news. Then he thanked me."

Our waitress hustled to our table with two pieces of key lime pie. Jill raised her hand, "I don't have room."

"They're on Sheriff McDowell. He paid for your dinners, too."

Jill ate a bite of pie. "I'm so full that I'm ready to pop."

I was halfway through my slice when the sheriff walked up to our booth. "I suppose Sheila told you I've paid for your dinners, but I wanted to thank you two for coming down to help Hawk with the investigation. I heard about what you two did at the van crash, and well, that was above and beyond."

I stood and introduced myself. "Thanks for your kind words but, it's Jill who was the hero."

McDowell smiled. "That's what I heard, but you're both good folks for jumping in to help like you did. The troopers and my deputies were overwhelmed, and you guys stepped in without anyone asking." He paused. "Are you making any headway on the surveyor investigation?"

"Not really."

"Let me know if I can be of assistance."

We thanked him again, and he moved to turn, but looked back. "Please don't measure the local people by those wannabe cowboys. There are a lot of people around here eking out a living who are the salt of the earth."

Jill nodded. "I'm from ranch country, and I know what happens when some cowboys get too much liquor in them."

McDowell laughed. "You handled yourself pretty well, Jill. Most women would've pretended not to notice them playing grab ass. You put Daryl right in his place."

"I hope Daryl and his buddies aren't waiting for us in the parking lot."

"No, they're probably parked on the side of the road, getting a ticket for DUI right now. I called it in when I paid for your suppers."

* * *

Jill was quiet on our drive back to the campground cabin. We were walking past the office when the door opened, and Jubal stuck his head out. "Sheriff McDowell called to make sure you made it back okay."

I laughed. "We're good."

"I turned on the lights for you and put some fresh towels in the bathroom."

Jill grabbed my hand and pulled me close as we walked toward our cabin. "There are some nice folks here."

"And like everywhere else, there are some jerks."

We were surprised by the cut flowers on the small table. Jill opened the tiny gift envelope on the plastic wand and read the card. Her eyes got teary, and she handed the card to me.

*Thanks for being our heroes. Matt and Mandy*

Jill sat in a chair and looked stunned. "I never sent anyone flowers when I was a park superintendent."

I opened the little refrigerator and took out a beer and the half bottle of wine left from the previous night. I poured wine into a plastic cup and carried it to Jill. "I bet you never had a ranger save the lives of a couple drowning kids."

She took the wine from me and sipped it. "I need to leave that behind for a while."

"The memory of times like this fade fast. Revel in it while you can."

"It's like the Hulett shootout. I want it put away."

"It's nothing like the Hulett shootout. We saved lives this time. That's a treasured memory."

Jill emptied her cup and held it out for a refill. "How did you get so wise?"

"I think it was the same stupid luck that brought us together."

"For a man who tastes his boot as often as you do, sometimes you say the most romantic things. If I were single, I'd suspect you were trying to get me into your bed."

I slid my chair next to her and nuzzled her neck. "Who says that's not my motive?"

"Hold that thought for five minutes while I take a shower."

# Chapter 12

We drove to the Everglades City restaurant that Hawk had taken us to previously. After ordering, Jill pulled out her new phone. "I've got to show you all the things this phone can do. I connected to the restaurant's Wi-Fi, and now I have access to the internet."

I feigned interest as Jill flipped through the features with the sweep of her finger. "It's lightning-fast and refreshes screens as quickly as I can move my finger. I can download and watch television shows or movies, and I've got instant access to Facebook, Snapchat, and Twitter."

"I hate to interrupt, but we need a plan for the day."

"We need to find out who's paying for the protesters.

"When did you decide that?"

Jill gave me *the look*. "Last night, after we fooled around. You fell asleep and started snoring. I thought about the case."

"What happened to post-coital snuggling?"

"I snuggled and thought while you snored."

"Did you decide how we could find that information?"

"I don't have the benefit of your experience."

Our breakfasts arrived, my ham and cheese omelet and Jill's oatmeal. "I wonder if the group who's filing the lawsuits to stop the drilling is involved?"

"That seems logical. How do we find out who settled the lawsuits?"

I salted and peppered my omelet, then took a bite. "Lawsuits are public information."

"Cool! I'll look it up on my phone."

"It might not be that easy. An environmental group may have filed the suit. We may have to find out who the directors are, and maybe even identify the big contributors."

Jill punched keywords into her phone as she ate her oatmeal. "Save Big Cypress LLC filed the suit, and Preston and Manger is the law firm who argued the suit."

"The lawyers won't tell us anything because they're bound by lawyer-client privilege. Look up the LLC."

"They're website lists an address and phone number in Florida City, but there's nothing about the directors or donors."

"Go to the Florida Secretary of State's website. The LLC is probably registered with them, and it usually lists the directors."

"How do you know all this stuff?"

I smiled. "My vast law enforcement experience has taken me many places."

"Okay, there are seven people listed as directors. Now what?"

"Google them. Find out who they are."

Jill flipped through screens on her new smartphone while I ate my omelet and toast. Absorbed by what she was seeing, she pushed her oatmeal aside. "Give me your pen and napkin."

I dug a pen out of my pocket and a spare napkin from the holder on the table. "What are you up to?"

Scribbling notes on the napkin, she glanced between her phone and the notes. "I've got too many screens open, and I'm losing track of where I've been and what I'm seeing."

"What are you seeing?"

"The directors of Save Big Cypress LLC are interlinked. They're all on Facebook, and they've all 'friended' each other."

"What?"

"Here," she said, spinning her phone around so I could see it. "I've got Facebook pages open for four of the directors, Jake Pope, Rhonda Fleming, Terrance Potts, and Theresa Collins. They're all Facebook friends, along with hundreds of other

223

people. Jake Pope lists his current position as an environmental lawyer, and Rhonda Fleming says she's an environmental activist. Terrance Potts is a professor of environmental studies, and Theresa Fleming is a science teacher in Miami."

"That's interesting, but what does that information do for us?"

"I've looked at their friends list, and they're all interconnected. Do you remember Robyn, the woman with the black eye? Here's her picture. Her name is Robyn Langer, and when I click on her picture, I get to her home page." The screens flashed, and suddenly, I was staring at Robyn sitting with a group of friends in a bar. Jill clicked again, and Robyn's personal information popped up. "She's in a relationship with Sean Beaupre. When I page down her friends list, here's a picture of Sean, one of the protesters we saw with her at the drilling site."

"Okay, we know they're all interconnected, and I'm not surprised by that."

"Robyn is a student at Alta Vista College in Homestead, and that's where Terrance Potts is a professor. When I page through her friends, I find...Bella Sanchez. We met her at the house where the protesters are staying."

I started getting into the flow of information. "What does Bella say about herself?"

"She's happily divorced and currently unemployed."

"Kai said she was paying him. How does she do that if she's unemployed?"

Jill spun her phone around and whipped through screens. "I'm searching her name, and she's got a home address in Fort Lauderdale. I'll paste the address into another search and...viola!" Jill paused. "Either this is a mistake, or Bella lives in a mansion on a canal."

Jill handed the phone to me, and I saw an aerial photo of mansions lined up along canals. When I zoomed out, I saw the canals all connected with the ocean. "That would explain how she can afford to pay Kai." I handed the phone back to Jill. "Is Kai listed as anyone's friend?"

Jill paged through Facebook, shaking her head. "He's not on Facebook at all. Let me run a different internet search on 'Kai' and 'security.'"

She turned the phone and showed me a picture of Kai, standing among a group of equally beefy men and a couple of women all in burgundy golf shirts with an embroidered logo. "This is the website for South Florida Personal Protective Services. They specialize in event security and bodyguard services."

"Kai's services can't be cheap, especially not if he's being paid for weeks of his presence at the house."

Jill took the phone back as the waitress refilled our coffee cups. "Are you through with your oatmeal, ma'am?"

"Yeah," Jill said without looking up. "Could I have a couple pieces of whole-wheat toast and some jelly?"

"Certainly," the waitress replied as she gathered my plate and the bowl of oatmeal.

"Look at this," Jill said, spinning the phone around. "Bella is all over the south Florida scene. There are pictures of her at dozens of fundraisers from food shelves to the Salvador Dalí Museum in St. Pete."

"What's the significance of that?"

Jill glanced at me as she paused. "Non-profits invite VIPs to fundraising events with the expectation of big donations." She spun the phone around again and pointed at the faces in a picture. "Here's Bella at a scholarship fundraiser, and she hardly resembles the woman we saw at the protesters' house."

The picture, taken a few years earlier, showed Bella in a long gown with a plunging neckline. Her hair was beautifully coiffed, and her necklace looked like it was diamond studded. "She cleans up nicely."

"The man holding her arm is the governor."

"So, she hangs out with the rich and powerful when she's not washing clothes and cooking for protesters. I wonder if her money came from her 'happily divorced' status?"

"Can I get y'all anything else?"

Jill was touching screens and preoccupied when her toast arrived. She shook her head without looking up.

I smiled at the waitress. "Just our bill, thanks."

"Please put some grape jelly on this for me." Jill pushed the toast toward me.

I checked the tiny plastic cups of jam. "It looks like strawberry or blackberry jam are your options."

"Strawberry."

After spreading the jam, I pushed the plate back.

Jill absently bit off a corner of the toast. "Bingo! Here's a society page article about Bella's divorce from Arnold Bach and calling her the heiress to the Sanchez orchards fortune."

"I'm not familiar with that family name."

After another few bites of the toast and a sip of coffee, Jill spun the phone around. "Here's an article about the family. It says they're the third largest orange juice producer in Florida."

I read the article as she finished her toast.

The waitress delivered our bill, and Jill paid her.

"It sounds like they've made a tidy fortune in juice and are now developing their orchards into senior living communities."

Jill wiped her mouth. "I recall a dispute over the boundaries of an orchard that's being converted into a golf course. You don't think...?"

"I think we need to talk to Bella again."

\* \* \*

We drove down the rough driveway to the protesters' house. A car was parked beside the back step, and a man showered under the black bucket by the outhouse.

Jill shook her head. "I couldn't be a hippie if it meant showering nude in the backyard."

The guy seemed oblivious to our arrival and lathered himself while we got out of the car and walked to the back step.

"He needs some meat on his bones," I said.

Jill made a point of not looking at the man. "Seems he could be modest enough to face away from us while he's scrubbing his..."

Bella opened the back door, interrupting our conversation. "Let me guess, you loved the tea and just had to have more. Please come in."

Jill scooted in the door without a look toward the outdoor shower, which made me chuckle. Bella looked at me and smiled. "You find our backyard shower amusing."

I nodded. "It pushes Jill's sense of modesty."

Bella motioned for us to sit at the kitchen table. "I'm more inhibited than many of our party. I shower after dark."

Jill sighed. "It'd have to be a new moon before I'd shower, even after sunset."

A young man and woman were washing and drying dishes in the sink. They chatted idly, acting nonchalant about our visit but seemed uneasy with sudden silences or over-the-shoulder peeks.

Bella took three mugs off the drying rack and dipped water out of a steaming pot into a teapot. "I assume it's not the tea that brought you back."

Jill took out her cellphone and showed the image to Bella. "Your dress was elegant."

Bella glanced at the cellphone photo of herself with the governor and laughed. "Siriano gowns don't really fit in here."

"Kai nodded toward you when we asked who was paying him," Jill said. "He literally meant it was you who was paying his salary."

Dunking a stainless-steel tea ball into the teapot, our hostess seemed to stall before she answered, "I don't see how that's germane to your investigation."

I slid a mug in front of me. "Someone killed the surveyors who were marking drilling leases. You're protesting the leases and apparently have the financial resources to…terminate their activities."

Bella's eyes darkened. "Like I said the first time you were here, we are peacefully protesting. I don't condone violence."

"What do you know about the orchard being sold to make room for a golf course?"

Bella carried the teapot to the table. The aroma of warm lemongrass wafted from the mugs as she poured. "I have no personal knowledge of a golf course being built on an old orchard. What makes you think I would?"

Jill ran her finger across the phone. Locating the screen she wanted, she held the phone out to our hostess. "This is you, the heir to the Sanchez orange juice empire?"

The dishwashers paused, waiting to hear the response.

"My family comes back to haunt me."

I sipped the herbal tea and let her incomplete answer hang in the air. "And…"

"And what, Ranger Fletcher?"

"Your family owns a lot of orchards that are getting converted into a 55+ retirement communities."

"The family does a lot of things that don't involve me. Do you know about everything your father does?"

"My father's been dead for decades. Jill or I speak to my mother almost daily."

"I'm sorry," Bella said, composing herself. "My brothers handle the family business. I'm a silent partner and not involved in the day-to-day activities of the family business."

"An orchard on the edge of the Big Cypress Preserve is having a property line dispute with a neighboring rancher. The missing surveyors marked the disputed property lines a few days before they disappeared."

"I don't know anything about that. Is it one of the Sanchez orchards?"

"We thought you could tell us," Jill replied.

"Like I said, I'm not involved in the operation of my family's business."

The back door opened, and the lanky man who'd been showering stepped into the kitchen. Jill looked away, then realized she'd seen a flash of denim when he'd walked in. "Ah, guests. I didn't recognize the car."

Bella smiled. "K.C., our visitors were admiring the outdoor shower."

"It's great. We fill the bucket from the pump, and the sun heats the water."

Jill smiled. "I think I use more than five gallons of water when I shower."

"Even where there's abundant water, like here in the Everglades, it's ecologically incumbent upon us to minimize our water consumption. We get wet, turn off the water, wash, then rinse. I don't even use half a bucket of water in one shower."

I nodded. "It would be even more efficient if two of you showered together."

K.C. laughed. "We've done that, but you have to be really good friends with the other person because you're bumping into each other under the tiny showerhead."

Jill held the mug up to hide her smile.

"I suppose that could cause some intimate contact," I said.

Bella put up her hand. "Let's not extend this conversation any further." She looked at me and asked, "Has that satisfied your curiosity on the orchard question?"

Jill was about to answer when I interrupted and asked, "Would you call your brother and ask if the orchard in question is part of your family business?"

"I doubt my brother knows."

"But you know who to call for an answer."

"I'll leave a message and ask them to get back to me with an answer."

"Can you make the call now, please?"

Bella stiffened, obviously unaccustomed to orders, no matter how politely they were proposed. She pulled a cellphone from her pocket and punched in a two-digit speed dial number. "Hector, a question has come up about the ownership of an orchard on the west edge of Big Cypress Preserve. Apparently, there's a disputed property line. Two National Park Service rangers are here requesting information." She listened for a moment, then added, "Please call me back as soon as you have the answer."

"Thank you," I said after she ended the call.

K.C wandered off with his towel over his shoulder. Bella looked at the dishwashing duo, then stood. "Let's continue this discussion out of this stuffy kitchen."

We walked halfway to the outhouse and stopped near the shower. "I don't want my...friends involved in my personal matters. I support them and what they are trying to do. I've tried to influence the actions of the family business without success. Instead, I use their money to fund things like this that irritate my brothers intensely." She smiled. "Just knowing the discomfort I'm causing for them is a small consolation for their continued draining of the water table, and the pollutants they spray on the orchards."

"How do you feel about the conversion of the orchards into retirement communities and golf courses?" Jill asked.

Bella blew out a breath. "I'm sure the water they consume and the pollutants they use are slightly worse than the orchards." Her phone rang, and she pulled it out of her pocket, then stepped away from us.

Jill watched her walk away. "I think she's being torn apart by the family business and her personal convictions."

"The waterfront property in Fort Lauderdale and the pictures of her at the charity balls make me feel like she's not suffering too badly."

"Give her a break, Doug. She's donating her money and time to the causes she believes in."

"She's not too serious about it."

"Why do you say that?"

"Her armpits are shaved. She's not a real hippie."

I felt the pain in my ribs before I saw Jill's elbow shoot out. "That hurts!"

"If you'd stop making stupid, snarky remarks like that, I wouldn't provide you with physical reminders of how stupid you're being."

Tucking the cellphone in her pocket, Bella walked back. "Our legal counsel reminded me that the parcel in question is outside the Park Service area and not subject to your jurisdiction." She paused.

234

"He said if I needed to show my good faith, I could tell you that land is owned by the Sanchez Family Trust. The trustees hired the surveyors to establish the orchard's boundaries."

"Thank you," I said. Then I offered my hand. "I appreciate what you're trying to accomplish, and I hope you're successful."

"Thank you," she said, shaking hands with both of us. "I often feel like I'm trying to empty the ocean with a teacup, but it's better than standing back and pretending I don't care. At least, I can sleep at night."

Bella walked with us to the car. She leaned on the roof after I closed the door and opened the window. "I hope that information is useful to you, and I assure you I didn't know about the orchard property line dispute."

"I think we need to talk to the rancher who's unhappy about the property lines."

Bella drew a breath. "Be careful. Some of the locals don't like outsiders snooping around and upsetting things."

Jill nodded. "We've heard that more than once."

"Just so you know, I'm laying all my cards on the table. I rent a motel room and shower when I go into Sweetwater to wash clothes. I feel the same way as you, Jill, when it comes to showering naked in the backyard. It doesn't matter if it's nighttime or not. It's just not happening."

"But you eat possum stew," I said.

Bella shuddered. "I eat the vegetables and leave the meat bits for the guys."

# Chapter 13

"Are we going back to Everglades City for lunch?" Jill asked.

"Hawk told me about the Miccosukee reservation while you were phone shopping. I think we should eat at their restaurant."

Jill stared at me. "Tell me they serve something besides alligator and frog's legs."

"Maybe your smartphone can pull up their menu."

Flipping through screens with the tip of her finger, Jill stared at the phone as I drove east. "Wow, they've got an eclectic menu with everything from gator bites to chef salads."

"Can I get a burger and fries?"

"That's on the menu, but you might want something...less calorie-laden."

"I like burgers."

"I watched you button your pants this morning, and it looked like they were a little snug."

"I'm sure we'll walk it off."

Jill's fingers flew through pages. "A typical cheeseburger and medium fries are 900 calories, and it would take 243 minutes of walking to burn that off. Were you planning to walk for four hours this afternoon?"

"Does the Miccosukee Restaurant have fried chicken?"

"That's even worse. A typical fried chicken dinner is 1,600 calories, and you'd have to walk continuously until dark to burn that off."

"If you say my only option is eating rabbit food, I'll sit at a different table."

"The menu is four pages long, and half the items are lower-calorie than a burger and fries."

"That means the good-tasting half is more than that."

"Deep-fried doesn't equal better tasting."

"It's a start," I replied. "I thought you weren't going to try and change me when we got married. That was part of the deal."

"You promised to love and cherish me, and I'd prefer if you would make food choices that extend rather than shorten our time together."

"Suggest something that doesn't have salad in its name."

"A grilled chicken sandwich and a cup of soup would have half the calories of a cheeseburger and fries."

I was working on a witty response when I realized Jill was dialing a number. "Who are you calling?"

She put up her finger and switched the phone to speaker mode.

"Hi, Jill. What's up?" Hawk asked.

"We're having lunch at the Miccosukee Restaurant. Would you like to join us?"

"I'm with a friend."

"Bring her along," Jill said. "It's Doug's treat."

Hawk laughed, and I heard a muffled conversation. "How soon?"

"We'll be at the turn in five minutes."

"It'll take us a little longer than that. Grab a table, and we'll meet you as soon as we can get free, in maybe ten minutes."

"It's a date."

"You know, it's his weekend off. He might not want to spend it with us," I said as Jill disconnected the call.

"He could've said no."

I sighed and shook my head. "Sometimes you're a real..." I considered what I was going to say and stopped.

"What's the matter, Fletcher? Did you get a taste of boot leather before the words all got out?"

239

"I love you."

Jill shifted in her seat to face me. "Uh oh. Was it going to be that bad?"

"No, I just thought I'd tell you how much I cared for you."

"Spit it out. What were you going to say?"

"Oh, look. I can see the sign for the turn."

"You know I'm assuming the worst."

"Did you see any salads on their menu?"

"I'm going to tell your mother you called me a pain in the butt."

"I never said that."

"Remember how I've been finishing your sentences? That's what was coming next, wasn't it?"

I parked without answering.

The restaurant had windows all the way around, giving even the indoor seating the feel of being outside. We asked for a table near the back and said we were waiting for another couple. "Two unsweet teas," I said.

"What's your plan for after lunch?"

"I saw a sign for airboat rides, and Hawk said there's a Miccosukee cultural center here."

Jill pulled out her phone and touched the screen. "I downloaded a map of the area beyond the west edge of Big Cypress Preserve, so the property line dispute must be in this area." She pointed to an area with few roads and even fewer houses.

"If the Sanchez family wants to build a retirement community here, they'll need big tracts of land for all the housing, recreation center, and pool. I wonder if they've offered to buy the surrounding ranches?"

"How would they do that without inflating the property prices?"

"I'm not sure, and I suppose they'd have a local lawyer or realtor contact the owners one at a time."

"It's a small town, and word would travel faster than they could make offers." Jill paused. "They'd need the county to rezone the land from orchards and ranches to residential, and that would alert everyone."

"I don't have an answer," I said. "See if there's a Florida criminal database. Maybe Butch Conley has a record."

Jill went from screen to screen, then keyed in something. "There's no Butch Conley, but there are half a dozen Conleys with recent records. I can narrow the search if you know what county he lives in."

"Everglades City is in Collier County. Try that."

"I've still got three Conleys. One is a teen and the second is seventy. Clarence Conley was born in 1989 and sounds most likely of the three." Jill touched the screen and took a deep breath. "Clarence is a

241

piece of work. He's got two DUIs and one assault conviction."

"He sounds like a fine, upstanding citizen."

Jill's fingertips flew over the screen. "I'm in the Collier County Sheriff's Department arrest database. It warns me that an arrest doesn't mean the person was convicted of a crime."

I snorted. "Yeah, I've arrested hundreds of people, and all of them told me they were innocent."

Jill stuck up a finger to silence me. "Holy shit. How often does a guy get arrested," she paused to count, "seventeen times for assault and only have one conviction?"

"Plea bargains to public drunkenness or disorderly conduct, dropped charges, reluctant witnesses, and more."

Jill looked up and quickly shut down her phone. "Our guests have arrived."

I stood and waited for Hawk and the young woman standing beside him to see me. Her hair was silky black, in two braids. She wore a bright yellow t-shirt, khaki slacks, and sandals. Hawk's transformation from ranger to civilian was stark, moving from Park Service green and gray to jeans and a white t-shirt. They made a cute couple.

"Alice, these are the rangers I've been telling you about, Jill and Doug Fletcher."

Alice's hand was dainty when we shook, and her smile was genuine and warm. "Cedric has rarely been as effusive in his praise of his Park Service colleagues. He was reluctant to meet you for lunch, but I insisted that he accept."

I chuckled. "I forgot Cedric is Hawk's name."

Hawk held out a chair for Alice, who sat across from Jill. "I'd hoped Hawk...Cedric would be willing to join us."

Hawk sat and looked uncomfortable. "Um, Alice teaches third grade at the Miccosukee school."

Jill's eyes sparkled, and her smile brought out her dimples. "When's the big occasion?"

I was lost for a second, then glanced at Alice's hand. An engagement ring sparkled on her ring finger.

"We're planning for a September wedding," Alice replied. "We won't be able to take a honeymoon during the school year, but that's the first time we can gather all our relatives."

"Your relatives aren't local?" Jill asked.

Hawk shook his head. "Alice moved here from Oklahoma. Her family is Cherokee."

She sighed. "It's impossible to trace my family tree, but our oral history says my forefathers lived in northern Georgia before the Trail of Tears relocations."

243

"How do you feel about life in Florida?"

"It's a lot greener, more humid, and less dusty than Oklahoma. Overall, I like it a lot." Alice looked at Jill. "You're from South Dakota?"

"I grew up on a ranch in the Black Hills, near Rapid City."

"I've heard it's beautiful there."

Jill nodded. "It is, but the winters are brutal. Doug and I are based in Texas now, at Padre Island National Seashore. It's about as hot and humid as it is here."

Alice looked at me. "Cedric said you're from the frozen tundra."

"Well, St. Paul is a bit south of the tundra, but yes, we get long cold winters."

"Rocky and Bullwinkle are from Frostbite Falls. Isn't that somewhere in northern Minnesota?"

"It's supposed to be International Falls, on the border with Canada. Car companies used to ship hundreds of vehicles there every year for cold-weather testing."

The waitress swept in with menus and took drink orders from Alice and Hawk while topping off our tea from a pitcher.

"What's good?" Jill asked, her eyes set on the three salad options.

"Fry bread is a traditional food that's…interesting," Alice said.

Hawk pushed his menu to the edge of the table. "I usually have the burger and fries."

Alice looked at him, then shook her head. "If I ate like him, I'd weigh three hundred pounds."

Jill laughed and closed her menu. "Doug could barely get his pants buttoned this morning after two weeks of burgers and key lime pie."

Hawk's eyes lit up. "The key lime pie here is better than at Joanie's Blue Crab Shack. Save room for a slice."

Glancing at Jill, I closed my menu. "I think I'll have the grilled chicken sandwich with a side of slaw."

"I'll split a slice of pie with you for dessert," Jill said, hoping to spare me from myself.

After ordering our food, Alice looked nervously at Jill. "You've been at a dozen different parks over your career. Are rangers required to relocate?"

"I moved for different experiences or to take promotions. There's no requirement that you relocate."

Hawk nodded. "Alice would like to stay here, where she's teaching. She asked me to consider taking a job with the tribal police."

"How do you feel about that?" I asked.

"There's not a lot of roads to patrol, and everyone I'd ticket or arrest will be a relative. I'm inclined to stay with the Park Service if they don't move me to a different state."

Jill looked at Alice. "He won't have to relocate. He can refuse a different posting."

Alice squeezed Hawk's hand. "I fear he'll get a posting that will be more interesting than this, and he'll want to take it."

I laughed. "That's a whole different problem."

"But the decision will be just as painful," Jill said. "We've struggled with the possibility that we'll be asked to relocate from Texas. We've put down roots, and I'm sure we'd decline a relocation offer."

"Cedric said you were a cop before you joined the Park Service, Doug."

"I actually retired, then Jill hired me as a law enforcement ranger. I discovered that I missed law enforcement."

Alice nodded. "The adrenaline rush."

"That, and the challenge of solving a mystery."

"And you, Jill, you were a park superintendent before becoming an investigator. That seems like an unlikely career move."

"There were a lot of factors in that decision. Not the least of them was falling in love with my best friend."

Our meals arrived, and the discussion shifted to the weather, the Miccosukee cultural center, airboat tours, and the virtues of the parks where Jill had worked. Alice was intelligent, intuitive, and a great conversationalist and Hawk let her talk, nodding his head and being agreeable. We split slices of pie, and I paid the check.

We stopped outside the restaurant door and shook hands. Alice held Jill's hand an extra second. "I've heard that heroes are unassuming, and you and Doug are as down to earth as any people I've ever met."

Jill blushed. "I'm not..."

Alice continued to clasp Jill's hand. "Someone once told me a hero is someone who takes action when every fiber of their rational mind is screaming at them to stop."

"That definition ignores the fact that no thought is involved."

"You just saw those kids in the van and dove into the water. No thought? No reservations?"

"Would you do any less if one of your students had been in that van?" Jill asked.

"I'd like to think I wouldn't, but I'll never know."

Jill squeezed Alice's hand and let go. "You would jump in without giving it a thought. I can see it in your eyes."

Hawk looked at me. "Now what? Are you going on an airboat ride?"

"It's up to Jill."

"I think we might drive by Butch Conley's house to see what it looks like."

Hawk's eyes locked on Jill. "Don't confront him."

"We'll just scope out the area."

247

Hawk reached out and placed his hand on Jill's shoulder. "Conley's a snake. Don't do anything unless you have some backup. Promise me."

Jill nodded.

We waved to Hawk and Alice as they pulled away. "They're a cute couple," I said.

"With so much growing up to do."

"So, what's your plan? Are we taking an airboat ride or touring the cultural center?"

Jill was deep in thought. "Let's see where Butch Conley lives."

"You just promised Hawk we wouldn't confront Conley."

"We'll just check out the neighborhood."

# Chapter 14

We talked about Alice, her heritage, and what an attractive couple she and Hawk made as we drove west on Tamiami Trail. With the sun past its apex, I flipped down the visor as we passed the Big Cypress Preserve's visitor center entrance.

"See if your phone will give us directions to Conley's house."

Sliding between screens with her fingers, Jill searched. "I loaded his address. Do you want a map, or would you rather have the phone tell us where to turn?"

"I'm a little creeped out by the electronic voices; just read the map and warn me before we need to turn."

My phone trilled but was deep in a pocket under the seat belt. "They'll leave a message."

"Matt gets irritated when you don't answer his calls."

The trilling stopped and was followed by a beep, indicating a message had been left. Within seconds, Jill's phone buzzed. She glanced at me. "I bet it's your mother.

She called you, and when you didn't answer, she dialed me."

"I won't bet against that."

Jill hesitated before accepting the call. "It's Hawk."

"Put him on speaker. He obviously wants to speak with both of us."

"Hi, Hawk." Jill eyed me.

"Doug didn't answer. Where are you guys?"

"We just passed the visitor center entrance."

"I thought you were going on an airboat ride."

"We decided to drive past Butch Conley's house."

"Is the county backing you up?"

"We're just driving past. We won't even stop."

Hawk sighed. "Grab a cup of coffee somewhere. I'll be thirty minutes behind you."

"It's your day off. We'll be fine."

Alice's voice came over the phone. "Hawk says we're going for a drive, and Cedric promised we'd eat at Joanie's. He's determined to make sure you're safe."

I leaned close to the phone. "We'll gladly have dinner with you, but you don't need to drive here because Hawk's worried about us."

"We're getting in the Park Service pickup," Hawk said. "Sit tight until we get there."

"We're not going to..." Jill looked at me as the dial tone hummed. "He hung up on me."

A chime sounded on Jill's phone, and she switched screens to see why she was getting an alarm. "Turn right at the next intersection."

I barely had enough time to brake hard and turn. The quick maneuver irritated the driver behind us, and he expressed his unhappiness with a hand gesture. His wife pointed out the children in the rear and expressed her displeasure with his angry display.

"Travelling with children is stressful," Jill said, watching the scene play out. She turned back to her phone. "Okay, follow this road for about three miles, then turn right again."

"Give me more than ten seconds' warning next time, dear."

Jill glared at me. "We could've left the voice directions activated, as I'd suggested, and the phone would've warned you ahead of the turn."

"Just give me a verbal warning next time."

"You didn't want the turn-by-turn directions." Jill looked back at the screen. "Okay, the next right will take us to an ell with a left turn. Conley's driveway is on the right about a quarter-mile after the turn."

"Can we drive past and make a loop back to the main road?"

"The road goes from solid red to dotted red past Conley's. I assume that means it turns from pavement to gravel at that point."

I turned onto a gravel road. "If this is a solid red line, I wonder what the dotted red line signifies?"

Our answer came as soon as we crested a hill. The road beyond Conley's driveway ended at a metal gate, and the trail beyond it was a rutted, muddy path through a pasture. "I've heard about mapping apps that lead people to dead ends."

"I think whoever mapped this had a sense of humor."

We turned into a driveway with a battered, rusty mailbox. A sign nailed to a wooden post said, *No Trespassing - Home Security by Smith & Wesson,* the message printed over a silhouette of a smoking pistol.

The surrounding land was a swamp and higher ground enclosed by a single strand of electrified fence. Two dozen brown cattle with white markings grazed lazily in lush pasture, their tails flicking continuously to chase away the flies and biting insects buzzing around them. A double-wide trailer sat alongside a dilapidated sway-backed farmhouse with peeling paint, missing shingles, and several broken windows.

"Doug, why would you move in a double-wide and not tear down the old house?"

"I think it reflects the lack of ambition displayed by the owners. It's probably too much work to tear it down."

A pair of coon hound mix dogs stood up on the wooden porch built onto the trailer. They bayed a couple times, then bounded down the steps. The hair on their backs was up, and their tails weren't wagging. They raced to our car, then trotted alongside it, one on each side.

"I don't like the feel of this. Back out and turn around."

"We're here. Let's see what plays out."

Jill watched the dog running beside her. "I don't want to get out."

"I think that's the message; stay in the car until the owner calls off the dogs."

The trailer door swung open, and a middle-aged man stepped out, wearing tattered jeans, a stained t-shirt, cowboy boots, and a straw hat. He spat a stream of tobacco juice toward the edge of the deck, then called the dogs. The hounds immediately loped to the deck and stood alongside the man, whose six-shooter and old-fashioned gun belt looked like it had come from the set of an old western movie.

253

I felt Jill's hand on my thigh. "His gun. It's just like the ones the guys in South Dakota use for quick-draw and western shooting competition."

"So?"

"The bullets we found where the surveyors disappeared were silver. Lead. The western shooters use cowboy loads— cast lead-alloy bullets with light powder loads. They have less recoil so that they can get back on target more quickly after a shot and reloaders save money by casting the bullets themselves."

I looked at the man's single-action pistol. "He's got an old six-shooter, and that'd be a candidate for a cowboy load." I paused. "How do you know things like that?"

"Daddy used to take Junior and me to the shooting competition, and I listened to all the guys talking about their guns, reloading, and the ammo."

"No wonder people thought you were a tomboy."

I expected Jill to jab me in the ribs for bringing up her painful teen years, but she didn't respond. I glanced at her and realized she was tense. She unfastened her seat belt, reached back with her right hand, and loosened her gun in the holster. Her breathing was quick, and her eyes were glued to the scene on the deck.

"Act nonchalant. This guy is a potential threat, but we don't want to escalate the situation."

Jill never took her eyes off the man. "We're not wearing vests."

"It's okay. We'll just ask him about the property lines and leave."

"Doug, I don't like this. Remember what Hawk said about the prickly people who don't like visitors."

"Shoot, shovel, and shut up."

"If this guy is a competitive shooter and things 'go western', he'll be able to shoot twice before we get our guns out of our holsters."

"Go western?" I asked.

"Think about old TV shows where a bar fight breaks out, and cowboys start shooting at each other over some verbal slight. That's 'going western.'"

"Take it easy. I'm just going to talk to him."

I got out, leaving the car door open. It left me a place to take cover if things *got western.* "Hi, we're from the Park Service, and we're looking for a couple of surveyors who disappeared. Have you seen their truck? We thought maybe they got stuck somewhere."

The man on the deck spat another stream of tobacco juice, splattering on the deck boards near the railing. "I ain't seen any surveyors."

"They had a blue truck with a topper. Have you seen it abandoned anywhere?"

The man made no move toward the steps, and his expression showed nothing but annoyance. "Haven't seen it."

I reached into my shirt pocket. "I've got pictures of them, a man and a woman. Maybe you've seen them walking on the road?"

The man put his right hand on the butt of the pistol. "I told you. I haven't seen them. I think you should leave."

I heard Jill's car door open, but I didn't want to take my eyes off the man's gun hand. "I'd appreciate it if you'd just look at the pictures."

"I'd appreciate it if you'd leave. You're trespassing on private property."

"Those are some nice-looking cattle," Jill said. "You've got better pasture than my family ranch in South Dakota."

"What part of trespassing don't you understand?"

"We're not here to make trouble. We're just trying to locate the missing surveyors. If we could just look around your property to see if we can find their truck…"

"I told you, their truck ain't here. I ain't seen them or their truck."

"Maybe it's shown up since you were in the back part of your property." I nodded toward the gate that blocked the road.

"Maybe they got turned around and drove into your pasture."

The cowboy squinted at us. "What kind of cops are you? You ain't got uniforms, and that looks like a rental car. I've never seen cops in a rental."

"We're National Park Service investigators."

"Park service cops. I ain't never heard of such a thing."

"We're federal law enforcement officers, just like a U.S. Marshal or DEA agent." I'd said the wrong thing.

The agitated cowboy snapped, "Huh. You're feds, and I ain't got no time for feds. It's bad enough we got local sheriffs snooping around, but now we've got G-men." The dogs reacted to the tone of his voice and looked up.

A hinge creaked behind us. I didn't want to take my eyes off the cowboy and dogs. In my peripheral vision, Jill turned to cover our backs.

A female voice behind me said, "Butch told you to leave, then said you were trespassing. You shoulda done what he said when you had the chance."

Jill whispered, "Shotgun."

I raised my left hand. "I got the message. We'll get in the car and leave."

The female voice said, "Uh-uh, Mr. G-man. You're going to drop your guns and cell phones on the ground and walk away from the car."

"Our office knows where we are. It'd be best if you just let us leave quietly."

The man on the deck drew his pistol and held it next to his leg. "No, you're trespassers, and we're protecting our property. Loreen, get the woman's gun."

I tried a gambit. "We're not going to give up our guns."

The woman's voice got closer. "You're giving up your guns? It's your choice whether you drop them or whether I take them while you're lying on the ground bleeding out."

"Okay," I said, stepping away from the car. I took the Sig out of the holster with two fingers and squatted down, setting it on the gravel driveway.

"Now step back and put your hands on the trunk," the woman said.

I turned and got my first look at Loreen. She was a big woman, near three hundred pounds, dressed in a loose shirt and jeans. Her finger was on the shotgun's trigger, and there was no hesitation or weakness in her eyes. I walked to the back of the car and put my hands on the trunk next to Jill.

"What's your plan?" Jill whispered.

"I don't have a plan."

"Shut up!" The woman yelled as the cowboy picked up my pistol. He looked at it, then tucked it into the waistband of his jeans, the dogs standing next to him, awaiting his command.

Smiling for the first time, the cowboy displayed a mouth missing five teeth. The rest were stained from years of chewing tobacco. "Since you can't figure out what trespassing means, we're going to put you to work. Loreen, get a couple shovels."

Jill's head tilted toward me and whispered, "Shoot, shovel, and shut up."

"Put your hands behind your heads and walk behind the barn."

When Loreen walked out the back barn door, she carried two shovels in her left hand and a double-barreled shotgun in her right. She led us toward the pasture then turned between the shop and barn, following us down a trail through the grass. Behind the barn, she dropped the shovels and stepped back. The cowboy was out of my sight, somewhere behind us.

"Pick up the shovels and start digging," he said. "Right next to those other dirt piles."

I looked to the right and saw two grave-sized dirt piles. "Are those the surveyors?"

Loreen cackled. "Just another couple people who didn't understand no trespassing and thought they could snoop around the backwoods."

"Create a diversion when we reach for the shovels," I whispered to Jill.

"Hawk will be here in ten minutes," Jill whispered.

"We'll be covered in dirt in ten minutes if we don't do something."

We approached the shovels, and the cowboy joined Loreen, standing a few feet to our left. The dogs seemed bored and wandered back to the house. The gun dangled from Butch's right hand but wasn't cocked. Loreen's shotgun was pointed at the ground. She grasped it ahead of the trigger guard, where it balanced, unprepared to shoot.

I reached down to pick up a shovel.

Jill cried out in pain. "My ankle!" She fell to the ground and grabbed her lower leg. With Loreen and the cowboy both tense and focused on Jill, I lifted the shovel. When it was near my ankle, I lifted my pant's cuff and pulled out the Smith & Wesson snub-nosed revolver I'd used as a St. Paul undercover cop.

The cowboy reacted to my move a second too late. My first shot hit him in the upper chest as he lifted and pulled the hammer of the single-action pistol. His gun was big and heavy, allowing me to fire a second shot that struck below his chin before he could aim at me. It must've hit his spine because his thumb slipped off the pistol's hammer. A shot flew past my ear when his brain signals stopped reaching muscles.

Loreen hesitated to process what had just happened. She switched the shotgun to her other hand as I swung the pistol toward her. She had the gun halfway to her shoulder. I took aim when a shovel flew through the air. Loreen was so focused on me she didn't react to the shovel until a fraction of a second before it hit. Her finger was on the trigger when it hit, but the gun was still pointed at the ground when it fired both barrels. A spray of wet black dirt erupted. Loreen lifted the gun toward me, but nothing happened when she pulled the trigger.

I aimed my revolver at her chest. "Put the gun down, Loreen. It's empty."

She pushed the lever that opened the breach, pulled out the two spent shotgun cartridges, and dug in her pocket, spilling a half dozen fresh ones on the ground. Jill sprinted ahead and hit Loreen in the solar plexus with her knuckles. Loreen's eyes went wide as air rushed from her lungs. She gasped for a breath. Jill pulled the shotgun out of Loreen's hands and prepared to swing it like a baseball bat.

"Stop! She's not a threat anymore!"

With fire in her eyes, and her veins full of adrenaline, Jill froze. My words made her pause for a second, and then she dropped the shotgun as I walked up. I kept my gun aimed at Loreen, who still struggled to draw a breath.

"Frisk and cuff her hands behind her. Make sure she doesn't have another weapon." I kicked the shotgun into the long grass, then kicked the cowboy's gun aside. I touched Butch's neck to make sure there wasn't a pulse, and then I pulled the pistol he'd taken from me out of his waistband. I was sure his heart had stopped when the second bullet hit, but I didn't want to be surprised.

Jill ran her hands over Loreen's clothing, emptying additional shotgun cartridges from her pockets. She spun Loreen around and cuffed her as Loreen continued gasping for breath. That task completed, Jill turned aside, placed her hands on her knees, and vomited into the grass.

We walked Loreen to our rental car and put her in the back seat. Jill turned to me. "What happened to my husband, who can shoot a smiley face on a target at ten yards? You hit that guy in the shoulder and neck. Where were you aiming?"

I held up the snub-nosed revolver. "Firing an automatic pistol at a paper target is different. Firing this double-action pistol at a guy who's shifting his weight while drawing a gun is *totally* different. I was also moving to make myself a harder target for him to hit when he got his gun up."

Jill got pale. "You mean hitting that guy in the neck was accidental?"

"Pretty much. If I hadn't broken his spine, he probably would've got six shots off at us."

"I'm glad I didn't know that before now."

"Let's look around behind the barn."

Jill raised her hands. "We're *not* going to dig in those other graves."

"That's a job for a forensics team. I just want to poke around to see what's out there."

Jill followed me past the fresh graves to a row of overgrown humps. She stopped and stared. "Do you think…?"

"Again, I'll let the forensics people decide how to check these out." I started walking, but Jill stood still, her back to me. "What's the matter?"

She turned, her face pale. "I just said a prayer."

After years as an agnostic, Jill embraced religion at our wedding. She'd encouraged our weekly attendance at the Episcopal church where we'd been married. That newfound religion led her to embrace God even further after near-death experiences in Wyoming and South Dakota. "You know I'm still a cynical cop, but I respect your need to pray."

She nodded, then embraced me. "You'll get there."

"I've seen too much…"

Jill pressed her finger to my lips to silence me. "You have to. You promised to

263

be with me for eternity, and that implies our souls being together."

"You're trying to keep me from going to hell?"

She released her hug and took my hand. "We're working on making a U-turn."

The pasture behind the barn ended at a sagging barbed wire fence. Beyond the gate was a hardwood hillock surrounded by a swamp. A crude gate, wide enough for a tractor, had tire tracks running through it. I unlatched the gate and led Jill through. "I wonder why anyone was out here?"

"Do we really want to find out?"

I ignored her reluctance and forged ahead into the wooded area. "Look at what's ahead of us."

Jill stood staring at the vehicle under a brown tarp. "It looks like a stripped-down pickup on cement blocks."

"I'm guessing Butch drove the surveyors' truck out here and was selling its tires and parts. We'll have to get the VIN off the frame and compare it to the surveyors' truck."

We approached the pickup, and Jill pointed beyond it. "There's a whole junkyard of vehicles back here."

I looked at the half dozen stripped cars and pickups, then felt sick. "I wonder if we've just solved some missing tourist cases?" I blew out a breath. "Let's get out of here. I think the county forensics team is going to have their work cut out for them."

* * *

Hawk and Alice arrived ten minutes later. Hawk was out of the truck with his gun drawn as soon as the vehicle stopped rolling. "What's happening? Where's Butch?"

I nodded toward the back of the barn. "He's dead."

Alice's eyes went wide, showing disbelief. "What? How?"

Jill put her arm around Alice's shoulder and steered her away from the barn, whispering gently. Hawk followed me behind the barn to the graves and Butch's body.

"Holy shit, Fletcher. How'd you get the drop on Butch? He's a quick-draw champion."

"Jill created a diversion."

Nearly an hour later, the first Collier County sheriff's deputy arrived. His Explorer raced up the driveway with lights and siren. I met him behind our rental car, holding up my badge. Jill leaned against the back fender with her badge clipped to her belt and her arms crossed.

The deputy stepped out with his hand on his pistol. "Did you make the call, 'officer needs assistance, shots fired?'"

I nodded. "We have a suspect in custody and another dead."

"Dead?" he asked.

I held out my S&W butt first. "Shot twice with my service revolver."

He accepted the gun, then made sure it was unloaded before putting it in his waistband. "Where's the deceased?"

I led him down the trail behind the barn and showed him the dead cowboy, pointing to his pistol in the grass. "He drew his pistol on me, and I got two shots off as he fired his gun. His wife's shotgun discharged into the ground over here. My partner disarmed and cuffed her."

The deputy stared at the dead cowboy. "That's Butch Conley. I'm having a hard time getting my head around you getting the draw on him. I've seen him put six shots in a silhouette's chest in eight seconds."

"My partner distracted him, and I had my gun up before he started to draw."

The deputy pulled on rubber gloves and picked up Conley's gun. He opened the cylinder, then looked up. "He got off a shot. Where'd it go?"

"I think it missed my ear by a couple inches."

"Where were you?"

I led him to the spot where I'd knelt, next to the shovel. "This is where he wanted us to dig our graves. I was kneeling here."

The deputy lined up the spots where Conley and I had been and walked to the barn. He put his finger on a spot about waist-high. "Fresh splintered hole right here in the siding. Conley's shot didn't miss you by much."

He walked back to the spot where Jill dumped the shotgun cartridges from Loreen's pockets. "Your partner, that woman in shorts, disarmed a woman with a shotgun?"

"My partner threw a shovel, then took the shotgun away from her."

The deputy looked at me skeptically as another siren whined in the distance. He walked to Conley's body. "Did you do CPR on Butch after you shot him?"

"His spine is broken. His heart stopped when the bullet hit him, and it wasn't going to start again."

He looked around. "Why were you behind the barn?"

"Like I said, Butch and Loreen handed us shovels and brought us here to dig our own graves."

He looked skeptical. "Say what?"

I pointed to the shovel and the two nearby areas of disturbed earth. "I suspect the two missing surveyors are buried there."

The deputy's eyes went wide. He took off his hat and ran a hand through his thinning hair. "Holy shit!"

267

"There are more mounds beyond that and a whole graveyard of stripped-down cars and pickups in the woods. Your forensics people are going to have a field day."

The deputy blew out a deep breath as he looked at the fresh graves. "I think they'll have nightmares if what you've said is true."

The second siren died as another sheriff's car raced up the driveway.

We walked back between the buildings. Jill still leaned against the rental car, now chatting with a female deputy sheriff.

"You guys will have to come to the courthouse and make statements."

I nodded. "We'll need to get an assistant federal attorney involved, too."

The deputy stopped. "Why get the feds involved?"

"The surveyors were killed in the Big Cypress National Preserve. And Butch and Loreen kidnapped and assaulted my partner and me. We're federal law enforcement officers."

"I think the state attorney will want to look at this first if those are graves in the back."

I shrugged. "Makes no difference to me. Let them fight out the jurisdictional battle. Either way, Loreen will go to prison for the rest of her life."

# Chapter 15

We were finishing the last of breakfast when Sheriff Ralph McDowell walked into the café. Nodding to me, he poured himself a cup of coffee. After placing his Stetson on the extra chair, he shook Jill's hand.

"Loreen Conley's singing like a canary. I can't believe *you* disarmed her with a shovel."

Jill smiled and wiped her mouth with a napkin. "The shovel was the only weapon I had."

McDowell shook my hand while shaking his head. "And *you* got the drop on Butch. That's really something. He's the county quick-draw champion."

"I was lucky to hit him with that little snub-nosed revolver."

The sheriff sat down and became somber. "The pickup truck in the woods does belong to the survey company. The coroner says the two bodies we recovered from the fresh graves are a man and woman who died of gunshot wounds. He got dental records overnight and confirmed the victims are the two surveyors."

Jill pushed her plate back. "Are there other graves?"

The sheriff looked around to make sure no one was close enough to hear him. "There are more, although we're not sure exactly how many. Most of the vehicles in the back were missing rental cars, so we assume we'll be identifying tourists."

Jill cocked her head. "Why?"

The sheriff drew a deep breath and blew it out. "It's hard to say. Butch was very protective of his land. You saw the sign on his driveway about shooting trespassers. Well, I think that's part of it, but he and Loreen were living off the land, and I suspect she'll tell us they were stealing cash and jewelry from the tourists and that Butch sold off car parts to shops that didn't ask too many questions."

Jill glanced at me. "My cynical husband thinks people are sometimes killed for their wallet or watch."

The sheriff nodded. "He's right. Some folks aren't quite right in the head and are willing to kill without remorse for a few bucks."

"Sociopaths," I said.

"That's the technical term. I think of 'em as crazy buggers." The sheriff finished off his coffee and stood. "I have to notify Terri Ortiz's family, and I'd like you to come with me in case they have questions. She's divorced, but her husband and his new wife are meeting me at Terri's house."

We followed the sheriff to Ortiz's home, where we were met by her ex-husband and their two teenagers, a boy and girl. His new wife held an infant. Holding his hat in hand, the sheriff gave Terri's husband confirmation that the dental records matched, leaving him shocked. The teens looked more curious than upset.

The sheriff stepped back and nodded toward us. "Our Park Service friends Jill and Doug Fletcher located her grave yesterday."

The new wife walked away, looking more angry than sad. Terri's ex-husband was in shock. The sheriff shook his hand, then walked away, leaving us with the grieving husband.

"Was Terri..." Words escaped him, and his eyes got teary.

"She'd been shot and buried in a shallow grave. She died instantly." I had no idea how quickly she'd been killed or what terror she might've experienced before the killing shot, but he didn't need those details.

He nodded and stared at his shoes. I heard his wife yelling at the children in the background. "Thanks. At least, we'll get closure. The twins probably won't grasp it for a while, but they'll know what happened. My wife's been telling them Terri ran away because…" he shrugged as his words were lost.

The woman with the toddler stalked down the hallway. "Your half-breed kids are making a mess in the kitchen." She took a breath, looked at us, then dismissed our presence as irrelevant. "I'm not raising those brats. Call their grandmother and tell her they're moving in with her." She stalked off again.

"I'm sorry. Giselle is wound a little tight. She'll calm down after the funeral."

With nothing else to say, we shook hands.

Jill and I walked to the car and climbed inside. I started it, letting the air conditioning run. Terri's ex-husband and his wife were in the midst of a heated discussion at the front door.

"Doug, the teens are only kids, and they haven't done anything wrong. That witch wants to farm them out to their grandparents."

"It's not our problem. The court will sort it out." I pulled her into my arms. "They have a loving father and grandparents. They don't need us to interfere."

Jill took out her cell phone and entered a number as we drove away. She spoke softly to Mandy Mattson, describing the confrontation with Butch, the fear she'd felt, and Butch's death. The conversation turned to the twins with the evil stepmother. After reassuring words from Mandy, she disconnected and dialed another number.

"Hi Liz, I hope I'm not catching you at a bad time." Jill nodded a few times, then explained our incredible week to Liz, a former ranger, who'd reported to Jill in Flagstaff and was now a friend and confidant. Something Liz said caused Jill to sit up straighter and brighten. She set the phone on the console and touched the speakerphone.

"Hi, Doug."

I pulled to the shoulder of the road. Liz became part of our lives when we searched through northern Arizona, looking for the origin of a drowned hiker. Liz and her husband, Jamie, bought my Flagstaff townhouse and were about to have their first child. "Hi, Liz. How are you doing?"

"I'm fat and tired and pee a little every time I sneeze. Everything Jamie does or doesn't do irritates me. Other than that, I'm fine. Jill said she pulled you out of peril and solved the mystery of some missing surveyors."

I laughed and looked at Jill. "I feel like I played a small role in sorting out the case."

"Hang on for a second. Jamie just came in, and I'm putting the phone on speaker." There was a pause, then Liz came back on. "Jamie's here. Say something to Doug and Jill."

273

Jamie, ever the minimalist, said, "Hi."

Liz waited a beat before coming back on. "Jill's call is timely. Jamie and I have been doing a lot of soul-searching as we've gone through the pregnancy. We've decided to continue living off the reservation. We want the baby to know his Navajo heritage, but we're going to raise him in Flagstaff and send him to public school."

"You know the baby is a boy?" I asked.

"The last sonograms were definitive."

Jill leaned toward the phone. "Have you considered names?"

"We're still working on that. I think we'll decide when we see him."

Jill looked at me and smiled. "That sounds like a plan. When are you due?"

"I'm scheduled for a C-section next Thursday."

"Wow, that's very specific—nothing left to chance," I said.

"There are medical reasons I won't get into, but yes, we have a specific date." Liz hesitated. "Um, there's something else we've discussed. Jamie, tell them."

"We're going to baptize the baby in the Lutheran church. Are you guys willing to be godparents?"

Jill snatched the phone off the console and held it in front of her. "Yes! We'd be honored to do that. Tell us when and where you schedule the baptism, and we'll be there." Smiling, Jill looked at me like she was about to say something that'd irritate me. "If it's okay, I'll fly back to spend a couple weeks with you after the birth to give you a hand."

"My mom is flying in for the birth and is staying for a week. I might appreciate some help after she leaves."

I took the phone from Jill. "If we can be helpful, let us know. We won't impose ourselves on you if we'd be a burden or in the way."

Jill took the phone back. "I want to see the baby, so I'll be flying in. If I can be helpful, I'll spend weeks there if I can help. If I'm in the way, I'll get a motel room."

"Thanks. Jamie and I will talk about it and let you know."

Jill ended the call and put the phone in her pocket, so I pulled back on the highway. Jill stared at me.

"What?" I asked, knowing she had a question for me.

"We're going to be godparents. Are you ready to make a few Flagstaff trips for the baptism and birthdays?"

"I think you'll have fun shopping for Christmas presents, too."

Jill put her hand on my leg. "I'd like it if they let him visit us in Texas when he's old enough."

"I bet he'd rather visit a South Dakota ranch and ride a horse."

"I think his godfather would have to ride along."

"I suppose I could learn how to saddle a horse."

Laughing, Jill put her head on my shoulder. "You have to put the bridle and saddle pad on first."

"I am marginally trainable."

Jill became very still, and I felt her body tense. "We almost died at Butch's ranch. I'm going to have nightmares."

"You reacted perfectly, and we're unscathed. We'll continue living every day and planning for a better tomorrow."

"I want to buy a house, someplace that feels permanent and is ours."

"You want to put down roots."

"Yes, I'm tired of being a vagabond. I want to put clothes in my own closet and dresser and I want to invite friends and family over for holidays." She paused. "I want a set of nice dishes in a china cabinet and pictures I've chosen to hang on the walls."

"I'd like those things, too."

"What else would you like?"

"I don't need a lot more than you beside me." I paused. "Do those things mean you're ready to retire?"

"Finding the surveyors' graves was sad, but I felt really good about giving their families closure. And being scared half to death at Butch's made me feel alive. No,

I'm not ready to retire." She turned to me. "Are you ready to retire?"

"I'm not ready for gardening and a rocking chair yet. Ask me again in a couple of years."

## The End

2020 #1 Bestselling Author
**Dean Hovey**

Dean Hovey is the award-winning and best-selling author of three mystery series. He uses his scientific background, extensive research, and several consultants to add reality and depth to his stories. One reader said his characters are like people he'd want to invite over for a beer and discussion.

Hovey's Fletcher mysteries follow U.S. National Park Service investigators Doug and Jill Fletcher as they solve crimes in a series of national parks and monuments, sometimes with a bit of humor and often with their evolving relationship. The Whistling Pines mysteries are humorous cozies set in a northern Minnesota senior residence, following Peter Rogers, the Whistling Pines recreation director, as he stumbles through the investigation of murders in his small town. The Pine County mystery series follows sheriff's deputies as they investigate murders in east-central Minnesota, dealing with crimes, criminals, and their own personal dilemmas.

Dean and his wife split their year between northern Minnesota and Arizona.

BWL Publishing

bwlpublishing.ca

www.ingramcontent.com/pod-product-compliance
Lightning Source LLC
Chambersburg PA
CBHW072355110726
47909CB00003B/711